AUGUST 9th

Stu Schreiber

AUGUST 9th

—ແ—

Stu Schreiber

27th Street Publishing
Del Mar, CA 92014

AUGUST 9th
Copyright © 2014 Stu Schreiber

27th Street Publishing
P.O. Box 354
Del Mar, CA 92014

ISBN: 1500906786
ISBN 13: 9781500906788

This book is dedicated to my wonderful friends,
Maureen & Rock Dime, Stan Silbert, Kim Fishman,
Connie Shaner, Cynthia Bolker & Greg Rizzi.

Introduction

Aug 10, Los Angeles Herald Examiner For one crazy night, August 9, 1969, Anaheim, CA, became the center of the rock and roll universe. Two British groups, fresh off the release of their second albums, blew the roof off the Anaheim Convention Center. A capacity crowd of 9,100, in a city best known for Disneyland, orange groves, and conservative politicians witnessed Jethro Tull and Led Zeppelin at their raw, energetic, explosive best.

With raucous fervor fueled by the heavy cloud of marijuana, Tull's front man Ian Anderson tripped around the stage with magical flute in hand as the band performed songs mostly from their new LP, "Stand Up." Most of the audience, unfamiliar with Jethro Tull, became enthusiastic supporters by the end of the set that was the perfect opening for what was to follow.

When Plant, Page, Jones and Bonham walked out they didn't just take the stage, they commandeered it and amped up the crowd into a hysterical frenzy. The standing, gyrating, screaming fans ignited Jimmy Page's guitar that fired right back with a performance somewhere between Hendrix and Clapton. Plant's rendition of "Dazed & Confused" was a vocal scream as his voice soared higher than the crowd. The more Zeppelin gave the more the audience gave back. The exhilaration was amazing.

By the time the band returned for their encore, "Communication Breakdown," the auditorium was euphoric. It was now one big party as everyone danced, yelled, screamed and stomped their feet to Bonham's pounding bass.

Every so often, we are lucky enough to watch greatness unfold before our very eyes. Last night, Jethro Tull and Led Zeppelin helped define rock greatness.

August 9, 1970

Dear Tess,

I hope this letter makes sense to you.

I'm not exactly sure why I'm writing you because I really don't know how to explain what happened at the Anaheim Convention Center a year ago today. Twice that night, for just a few seconds each time, our eyes met and I was overwhelmed by a feeling I've never felt before. I apologize if you're not sure what I'm talking about, but you're the only person in the world who might be able to tell me what happened. Was it something caused by the emotions from the unbelievable concert? Did Led Zeppelin's pounding beat and the pot filled arena affect me or us?

We never spoke but our eyes and the smiles we shared were, at least for me, totally overpowering and unexpected. It reached something deep inside me. I left Anaheim confused, trying to understand something I couldn't explain and my hope is that you can shed some light on what you felt—if anything.

Before I go any further let me explain that I discovered your name and address by accident. Although I can't erase the image of your beautiful smiling face from my mind, I assumed it would pass with time and you would always remain a mystery since the only information I had was your seat number, Section B Row 23 Seat E. That was easy to figure because I was in the row behind you, two seats to the right, or 24 C.

Then in March, I was having a burger with the boys in Westwood and a guy stops at our table and says, "Hey, that concert was outta sight!" At first I wasn't sure who he was talking to or what concert he was talking about. Then I realized I was wearing the concert t-shirt from Led Zeppelin. This guy's name is Mark and like me he's a Business major at UCLA, but he'll be a sophomore and I'm a junior. My girlfriend Maggie and his girlfriend Sheila are both Delta Gamma's, Maggie at UCLA and Sheila at USC.

Mark, who knew one of my buddies at the table, sat down and joined us and we relived the epic Zeppelin concert agreeing it was the best concert we'd ever seen. He went with a big group of thirty who were scattered throughout Section B. When I told him that's the section we were in I desperately wanted to describe you, but how could I explain you? I certainly didn't want to share the question or an answer with my friends at the table who all know Maggie. Before we left the restaurant

Mark and I talked about getting together for dinner or a concert with the girls.

In July, Maggie and I joined Mark, Sheila and several other couples for a Ten Years After/Grand Funk Railroad Concert at the Forum. Before the concert we started to relive Led Zeppelin and where everyone was seated. When Sheila said her friend Tess Davis was seated in Row 23, she got my attention. Then, when she described you, as her tall, beautiful blonde friend I just about spit out a mouthful of soda. Sheila also said you were a DG, too, but at UCSB. I fought off my curiosity and also the uncomfortable feeling of guilt I had with Maggie sitting next to me and quickly turned the conversation to Grand Funk.

After hearing you went to UCSB I immediately thought back to January when I drove up to the campus with some friends to check out the demonstrations against the insane Vietnam War. Nothing, nothing is more important to me than stopping all the killing. It was brought home even more when a high school buddy of mine, just nineteen, was killed there. Because he drew a low lottery number he decided to enlist. Shit, he couldn't vote but he could die for his country. I'm so lucky my lottery number is 347. I wasn't at Santa Barbara to witness the burning down of the Bank of America but if that's what it takes to stop the massacre of innocent victims then it's well worth it. Then Kent State goes off and four students are killed for protesting our invasion into Cambodia. The world led by

America is on tilt. What was it like for you during all the protests?

Speaking of a massacre, I still can't believe the Sharon Tate murders, which occurred on the same date as the Zeppelin concert. I'm glad the trial has finally started and hope justice is soon served. If a man can give the appearance of the devil it surely must be Charlie Manson.

That's enough of the killing talk. Back to why I'm writing this letter. Tess, I kept telling myself to let whatever we experienced go, but a day didn't pass without flashing on the vivid image of your eyes and smile and now you had a name. I kept searching—for some kind of explanation.

Finding your address was easy and only took a few phone calls. I gave the DG House in Santa Barbara the excuse that I found a little phone book of yours that must have fallen out of your purse and I wanted to mail it back to you. It was a comforting relief you're at UCSB reasoning the 100 miles between us is for the best.

For three months I thought about what to do with your name and address, and it always came back to the same two things. First, I didn't want to freak you out or have you think I was stalking you or was some kind of weirdo. My second thought was for Maggie, who I'd never cheat on. I justified writing to you would be okay since I didn't try to get your phone number and call you or just show up at the Delta Gamma house in Santa Barbara. I know my justification requires a rather humongous leap of faith.

I've started this letter a couple dozen times and I'm still not sure what to say or how to say it. I'm still searching and trying to explain what happened in Anaheim and why your image still remains so vividly clear. Yet, I don't know what I expect or want to happen by sending you this letter. It's also totally unlike me to write any letter which confuses me even more and probably explains why it's been so difficult to write.

I know I'm fishing but I'm still puzzled over what I'm fishing for. I only hope you can help explain what happened and why it remains such an overwhelming feeling and vivid memory. Could it have been the same for you? If so, have you experienced the same sensation before? Or, maybe you didn't feel anything? If nothing else, please accept this letter as a flattering gesture and accept my word that I will honor your privacy. I'm just searching for understanding.

August 9, 1971

Dear Tess,

I hope you received my letter and at least found it interesting and a compliment. I didn't make a copy but I remember most of what I wrote.

It's been two years since the Led Zeppelin concert and I've probably relived those few seconds when our eyes met a thousand times. I still don't know how to explain what happened or how your face can be so clear in my mind.

Speaking of concerts and music it's hard to believe Jimi Hendrix, Janis Joplin and Jim Morrison all died in the past ten months and all at twenty-seven. I never saw Hendrix but I did see and love Janis and the Doors.

I do remember writing you about my opposition to this insane Vietnam War. Thank God for Daniel Ellsberg and the New York Times and the release of the Pentagon Papers that clearly shows the brutality and dishonesty of our government. I guess the heat was turned up so hot Washington had no choice but to pass the 26th Amendment lowering the voting age to eighteen. Soldiers who can die for their country certainly should be able to vote. We'd have no wars if those leaders who send us to war had to physically lead the infantry charge.

Tess, I know I told you I'm a Business major but I'm not sure I told you what year. I'll be starting my senior year and if I can pull off the financial end of things I'm thinking of going to Stanford for my MBA. I went up there last month to check out the campus and surrounding area. Everything was very impressive and there seems to be so much energy and exciting things happening. There's also a bunch of new companies that are hiring almost every MBA graduate from Stanford. The big problem is I would be away from Maggie for at least a year. That's why I'm also considering UCLA and USC. No matter what I've got to take out a student loan. My parents still have my younger sister at home and I don't want them to pay for my graduate degree with Janet starting college in a year.

Strangely, I'm not sure what to ask you. I'd like to know so much more about you like where you're from, if you're in a relationship, what you're studying, and what you enjoy doing besides rock concerts and your sorority stuff. Then I quickly realize knowing more would really complicate things. Perhaps it's best you remain a mystery? I really don't know why I'm even sending you another letter since I didn't receive a response to my first. I know I'm talking in circles which is something I rarely do with my left brain logical mind.

Hope all is well in your world and thanks for taking the time to read my second letter.

Dan

August 9, 1972

Hi Tess,

Here I am, once again, and I still see you at least once a day.

Not sure at what point, or how many letters it will take to constitute a pattern or habit but for an unknown reason I look forward to writing and mailing you these letters. I did have a thought that it's entirely possible these letters are being sent to someone else, by mistake, and somewhere a seventy-five year old woman or twenty year old long haired hippie are laughing their ass off at this crazy, romantic business student who keeps sending very personal letters to a woman he's never met or even received a response.

Sadly I'll be saying goodbye to UCLA but it was the best four years of my life. The best part of my graduation was seeing the pride on my mother and father's faces. I was their baby and they witnessed each and every step of my journey, supporting me all along the way.

And graduating with honors sweetened everything and brought all three of us to tears. I only hope I inherited their wonderful parenting skills.

I'm excited to be going to Stanford for my MBA and found a little studio apartment about a mile from campus. It's going to be tough without Maggie but we'll work it out. I plan to fly or drive down to LA often and she can also come up here. The bigger question is what she does after she graduates in June. She's a psychology major and that probably means grad school. She's applied to a bunch of schools with Cal being at the top of her list. If that happens, and with her grades it should, we can rent a place between the two schools that are about forty-five miles apart.

Well, there appears to be two things we can count on, one bad and one good. The horrific war in Southeast Asia continues as our government feebly attempts to justify all the killing. On the good side, and on a much lighter note, we can depend on UCLA basketball which has now won an unprecedented six championships in a row. Don't think I've mentioned this but I played basketball in high school and was pretty good, for high school. I optimistically thought I could play at UCLA because I played there in a summer league.

Although I was offered a basketball scholarship at several schools, including UCSB, I decided to literally shoot for the moon and went to UCLA without any financial assistance. That meant I tried out as a walk-on. My first practice quickly brought me back to earth. Everyone was taller, faster and just better than me. It was a blow to my ego but in the long run it was probably the best thing that could have happened. I was able to concentrate on studies and at least met some unbelievable athletes and of course, the Wizard of Westwood, Coach Wooden.

I can't help but wonder what might have happened if I went to UCSB. Would we have met and, if so, would we have looked at each other the same way? Is that possible? The twist and turns of our lives are amazing.

Tess, I'm not sure when you graduate and I can only hope you'll have your mail forwarded to your new address. I'll understand if that presents a problem with a boyfriend or even your husband, but I choose to believe you will continue to receive and read my letters. However, should a letter be returned I'll understand and gratefully wish you a wonderful, happy and fulfilling life.

August 9, 1973

Tess,

Here we are again and I hope life finds you wonderfully happy.

Think you've probably graduated from UCSB and can't help but wonder what life holds for you? Then again, I hope my letters are actually reaching you. Your image flashes before me all the time and would create some very awkward moments if people could read the smile on my face when I see you.

Finally, finally we're done with that crazy war. First the Paris Peace Accords that provide a cease fire were signed in January and then our last troops left at the end of March. It's too little, too late, but it's about time and hopefully we've learned our lesson.

I just love Stanford and Palo Alto. If you're unfamiliar with the area it's the southern portion of the San Francisco Bay and actually a peninsula. The campus is called the Farm because it was built on the site of the founder's actual family farm. It's a very different environment from UCLA, much smaller, but even more stimulating with all sorts of exciting new technological innovation that has practical application for the real world. There's a feeling of being surrounded by big thinkers who push the envelope of conventionality and look for new instead of just better. People here really believe we're going to affect positive change and see Stanford as one of the top universities in the country.

Much of the credit for this atmosphere has to be given to the Stanford president, Richard Lyman. Against the War he also has a deep belief in academic freedom and free speech. He's been able to balance those positions with an unwavering opposition to violent protests and sit-ins.

Studies in my first year were about general management, more specifically, strategy, systems and leadership. My favorite course was in a seminar setting where we'd analyze and debate issues that arise in management situations. This year will be much more personalized. I'm particularly interested in the financial challenges of start-up companies, funding options and capital structure. I'm excited to start interviewing with companies based in the area and setting up that interaction is one of the things Stanford does just about better than any other college.

My neighbor, Jeff, is a graduate student in engineering. The stuff he's working on is well beyond my comprehension but what little I understand is fascinating. We joke about starting our own company, but that's not unusual because talk like that is all over campus. Jeff takes pride in being labeled a nerd. All I know is he's constantly working on something new and always has a Dr. Pepper in his hand. His apartment looks like a hardware store that was just hit by a tornado.

Another big difference between Stanford and UCLA is the surrounding area. UCLA has Westwood and the lurking behemoth of LA and a multitude of industries probably led by entertainment while Stanford acts as an informal hub for many new companies that are redefining how things are done. Thank God our mascot has been changed from the Indian to the Cardinal.

Last year was a real struggle without Maggie and although we talked every night it wasn't the same as being with her all the time. I'm going to tell you something I haven't told anyone else. I was studying on a quiet Saturday night in January when one of the cute gals who lives in my building came over to invite me to their party and also to see if I had any tequila. Next thing I know we're chugging down shots in my apartment. After I lit up a joint things got a little heated and we were all over each other on my small couch. Luckily I came to my senses when she started to unbutton my jeans. It took ten minutes to convince her she was super hot and I only stopped because I have a wonderful girlfriend I couldn't cheat on. Ironically, moments like that convince me even more how much I love Maggie. I can't help but question my judgment and how I could let things go that far. For obvious reasons I didn't make the party.

August 9th

Speaking of Maggie, she's getting her Masters at Cal and we found a cool apartment between the two schools in San Mateo. We're really closer to Stanford but it seemed like a better option than living in Hayward or Fremont. More importantly, we'll be living together for the first time. Actually, neither of us has lived with anyone before other than in the dorms. We've spent plenty of weekends and sleepovers together but I'm really excited to start our real life together. Of course I missed the sex last year but even more I missed her friendship.

I'm surprised it's not more awkward to write about Maggie in a letter to you but I can't escape how easy writing to you remains. Hopefully my writing skills are improving and I thank you for being part of such an everlasting memory.

Dan

August 9, 1974

Hi Tess,

After 19 years of schooling I'm finished unless I want to go back for a Doctorate which doesn't sound inviting.

Another graduation, another celebration and guess what, I've got a job. Can you believe it? I've got my first real job making real money and actually started two weeks ago.

My parents flew up for my graduation weekend. My dad, Carl, ever the engineer, always regretted not being able to get his Masters primarily because I was on the way and he needed to support a family. He seemed prouder than I've ever seen him and we shared our warmest hug ever. He also enjoyed interacting with my electrical engineering buddy and former neighbor Jeff. He actually understood Jeff's language which impressed the hell out of me. Of course my mom, Laura, and Maggie have always had a wonderful relationship with me being their favorite topic which can be awkward at times.

I think I mentioned Stanford's highly regarded career interviewing process. Now, after going through it, I can't praise it enough. It was interesting, compelling, challenging and exciting, especially when the companies would talk about who they were, what they did and where they were going. Choosing my prospective employer from the list of a half dozen companies that made me offers was difficult. Although I'm a numbers guy it ultimately came down to people. Who did I want to work for and with? In the end I narrowed the choice to two very different and very new companies, Atari and Kleiner Perkins. Atari invents video games and is just introducing a game called Pong. I got to play it at their new office, in Sunnyvale, and it's so cool, sort of an electronic ping pong game. Kleiner Perkins is this new Venture Capital firm. They fund other companies, primarily tech start-ups. The fascinating part of their business model is that they get to pick and choose between many new companies on the very cutting edge of new ideas.

Before I made my decision one of my professors recommended I meet with another company. Only it wasn't really a company, just yet. And, they really didn't have an office, just yet. In fact, they're still trying to decide what to call the company. This is a start-up in the truest sense of the word. Three Stanford engineering students, who never graduated, are working out of a garage in one of their parents' homes. They desperately need a business guy to help them with their finances including raising money. It's a little too far out for me but this type of situation is not that uncommon up here. I did have second thoughts about not trying to find out exactly what they're working on when I heard the professor who told me about them had joined their team.

In the end, I chose the company with the actual product, Atari. I think Pong could be the start of a new entertainment market. Their offices are only about 10 miles from Stanford which means Maggie and I have been able to stay in our apartment in San Mateo. Speaking of Maggie, she absolutely loves Cal and I have to admit the atmosphere there is electric. If Stanford is about innovation and money, Cal is sort of a consciousness incubator. I love them both but I also loved UCLA, so maybe I just love the college environment. Maggie and I really enjoy walking around Berkeley and Haight-Ashbury. This was and still is the center of the hippie, anti-war, free-love world and there can't be better people watching anywhere.

Getting back to my career, I can't believe it's all starting, right now. As you can tell I'm excited about my new life and actually being able to apply what I've learned to solve real problems. Or to quote my favorite professor, Rufus Sinclair, at Stanford, "Apply the applicable thought process to solve any specific challenge."

There's even more good news. With what I'm making I'll be able to pay off my student loans in about three years. I'll be glad to get that overhang taken care of since I might have even better news in the very near future.

Maggie and I really love living together. Since she's my best friend I'd rather hang out with her than anyone and we really are compatible. She's much easier to live with than me. Her patience and wonderful perspective help balance my impetuous nature. Although we're not engaged, just yet, it may happen soon.

Gosh, I've written seven paragraphs all about me which is interesting because in business I've learned to use the pronoun "we" instead of "I" whenever possible. I'm not sure that's relevant and what I'm trying to say is, how are you? I know that's a question I'll probably never receive an answer to but I really hope you are happy, healthy and excited about your future. I did get a notice from the post office of your address change. Although I've never been to Boston I can't help but wonder if you're going to grad school or doing something else. Tess, I still see you every day and in my rapidly changing life you remain a wonderful, beautiful constant.

Wow, I just heard the news that Nixon resigned today. Guess he realized impeachment was a certainty and chose to leave on his own. I guess that ends this letter on a high note. Good riddance Dick.

Dan

August 9, 1975

Hi Tess,

It's been such a crazy busy year that I don't know where to start, but since work's been the biggest change in my life I'll start there. It's been overwhelming, exciting, stressful and rewarding. There is no such thing as a 40 hour work week. My week is more like 70-80 hours or, as Maggie consistently reminds me, way too much. This whole geographical area is in play, meaning deals, deals and more deals. Meetings and phone calls consume most of my days. Paperwork and preparation for the meetings fill up my evenings. I love the days much more than the nights which too frequently keep me in the office till midnight. The Company is working on all sorts of great new products like video game consoles and compatible computers.

My role is to provide a financial analysis of potential deals and new products. Is it a good deal or product? Will we make money and how much? It sounds pretty simple but gets awfully complicated very quickly. There's always a wild card that hovers over everything. That card is everything always seems to be for sale, including the company, if the price is right. It's the culture of this tech industry. Build, sell and then build something new. Job security is offset by the huge returns for the owners of the companies, either public or private. Getting to that sweet spot is my objective.

Unfortunately, there are only so many hours in the week and work takes me away from Maggie far too often. She's been very understanding and more concerned about the toll it takes on me, but we both agree that now, while we're young, is the time to go for it. Plus it seems like the best investment we can make for our future.

Although work has been the biggest change in my life it hasn't been the most eventful. April 26th is Maggie's birthday and I suggested we fly down to LA that day which happened to be a Saturday, check into a hotel, have a nice dinner and then go see Pink Floyd at the LA Sports Arena. Then on Sunday we could visit our families. Since my family lives in North Hollywood and Maggie's in Santa Monica, we could make both stops, visit with our parents and still get back to LAX for our flight home Sunday night.

It sounded like a fun weekend, but I left out a few details. First, we weren't visiting both families on Sunday. Although I said her folks would be our second stop it was our only stop. I spoke with her parents and mine a month before and set up a surprise birthday party for her at 1:00 pm on Sunday. Since her actual birthday was the day before I didn't think she'd expect a party, especially not a surprise party, the next day. Her parents helped me with a guest list and I added a dozen other names. Oh, there was one other little surprise, our engagement. Maggie and I constantly talked about getting married when the time was right. Well, I thought the time was right, and her surprise birthday party seemed like the perfect opportunity.

Sometimes I really appreciate tradition and a week before her birthday, while Maggie thought I was at work, I flew down to LA and met with her parents to ask for their blessing to marry their daughter. Not surprisingly, they had an idea I wasn't there just to discuss the party arrangements and proudly gave me their blessing. I called my parents with the news from the airport just before my flight took off.

One of the guys from the office recommended a jeweler and I picked out a ring in about twenty minutes. Maggie is so unpretentious I knew she'd appreciate anything I gave her but since this was the only engagement ring I'm ever going to buy, it was time to splurge. I did my best not to give anything away the week before the party and even came home from work at 6:30 one night so we could do a little shopping and Maggie could pick out something new to wear for the weekend. I like to think I know a little something about women.

The weekend was a smash hit and a double surprise for Maggie. She was totally unaware of what awaited her as we walked into her parent's house. The expression on her face, when fifty guests jumped out from every-where and yelled "surprise," was wonderful. About an hour later I grabbed a half filled champagne glass and tapped it with a spoon to make a toast. I asked Maggie to join me where everyone could see us and I proceeded to toast her birthday. Then in the middle of my toast I knelt to one knee, pulled out the ring from my pocket and asked Maggie to marry me. I'm not sure who started to cry first. All I remember is her shaking her head up and down and saying yes, yes, yes. Now we really had something to celebrate. There was a wonderful moment a little later on when Maggie and I were joined by both sets of parents. They told us how proud they were of us and the responsible adults we'd become and we told them how blessed and thankful we were to have them as parents. Moments in life don't get any better.

As for our wedding it looks like next June. Now that Maggie has her Masters in psychology she has a big decision to make. What does she want to do? Her options include teaching, therapist or research and that may mean even more school. We'll see.

I forgot to tell you about Pink Floyd. They were so rad, especially the second half of the concert which fea-tured songs from The Dark Side of the Moon. I've never heard music quite like it before. Incredibly, they per-formed five concerts on consecutive nights at the Sports Arena. There were fans around us who loved the group so much they bought tickets for all five.

Tess, I'm not sure I'll ever go to another concert without seeing you. Strangely, even though I've written about my new job and my engagement it doesn't seem to affect my reality as it relates to you. I know that probably sounds crazy but you seem to be separate from everything. I hope you're happy, healthy and living your dream.

Let me close by saluting one of my heroes. Coach Wooden retired after winning his 10th National Championship in March. I think I only had two conversations with him but the last has always stuck with me. He told me, "Never, ever be afraid to fail." Thank you, Coach.

Dan

PS: As I finish this letter I reflect on the process for writing you a letter each year on the anniversary of the Zeppelin concert. Each letter forces me to prioritize events from that year, but I'm not sure I accurately convey the emotions I feel at the time the event occurs. Plus subsequent events often change my perspective. Now I can appreciate a diary, and only hope my writing isn't boring you. Please understand after six letters I'm still confused about us.

August 9, 1976

Dear Tess,

We did it! We got married on June 19th, in a little church in Santa Monica.

Although Maggie and I are not religious we went along with our parents' wishes and had the ceremony at a church. The reception was about five miles away at a private beach club. (Maggie's parents are members) We had about 175 guests at the reception with an open bar, a buffet dinner and dancing until midnight with a local band, and later a DJ.

I don't remember much of the day, but luckily we have plenty of photos to refresh our memories. One of my ushers insisted I take a couple hits off a joint to calm me down before the ceremony and also found me for a few more hits before dinner. When I mix in all the alcohol I guess it's not that strange my memory is so hazy.

Do you remember seeing Maggie at the Zeppelin concert? I ask because for some reason I feel a little uncomfortable talking about how she looked and what she wore. I'll just say she looked absolutely amazing. I had to wipe tears from my eyes when I first saw her coming down the aisle with her dad at the church. For our first dance we chose the Righteous Brothers, Unchained Melody. (We brought the album so we could have the DJ play the original version)

Unfortunately our honeymoon had to be postponed. It's become so hectic at work that I couldn't afford to take the time off. Maggie said she understood, but she always says she understands. I want to make it up to her with a great trip to either Hawaii or Europe.

Speaking of work, I won't be surprised if the Company is sold, soon. I normally know what's going on around here and I'm included in most discussions but that's changed in the last month. What I have received is requests for lots of financial information. Maybe I should have chosen to work at Kleiner Perkins?

Have you played Pong? Our alliance with Sears was a huge success. We projected to sell 50,000 units last Christmas and sold more than 100,000. We've also got lots of new stuff in the pipeline. If possible, I'm working even more than last year. There's just not enough time in the day to get everything done. Plus, every Wednesday evening I get together with a group of about a dozen other Stanford grads to discuss what's going on in the Valley. We network about job opportunities, new companies and the latest technology. We're split equally between the business and tech side of things and it gives us a chance to keep abreast of what's going on in the Valley.

Not sure if you remember me writing about Jeff, one of my neighbors at Stanford. He's the nerd engineering genius. I ran into him at a conference over the summer and he works for the Palo Alto Research Center which is part of Xerox and next to the Stanford campus. He's working on some really cool stuff including the Ethernet which is a system for connecting computers within a building using hardware running from machine to machine. At least that's how he describes it. He believes someday everyone will be connected and that's what his work is all about. The longer I work here the more I realize that Jeff and guys like him are the real drivers of technology. People like me just enable them to have the money and freedom to pursue the future. We call them far out or crazy until they come up with something that will change the world. At Stanford we used to joke about starting our own company, but today I think of it as potentially a great opportunity. Jeff's a genius.

We also flew down to LA in June for my sister Janet's graduation from UCLA. She was a history major which probably means law school. I don't think she's ever gotten anything but an "A" in every class she's ever taken. Besides her natural intelligence she has an unbelievable study ethic, certainly way beyond mine. She's also a better athlete than me although I'll never admit that to her.

Everything seems to move so quickly up here and not just business. Maggie and I are already talking about kids and buying our own home. They seem to go hand in hand. We agree on two children, but Maggie's torn between pursuing a career and staying home to raise our family. I'm leaving that decision to her and will support whatever she decides. Interestingly, my mom worked most of my childhood while Maggie's mom did not.

Tess, you're still with me, everywhere, all the time. Despite all that's happened in my life you are unique in what you represent and for that I remain grateful and hope you are flourishing.

August 9, 1977

Hi Tess,

I was right.

Atari was sold in October of last year to Warner Communications. The sale price was $32 million. I stayed until the end of the year while I interviewed with five companies. That's when the networking I've been doing really paid off. It was a very different process from the interviews I had coming out of Stanford. This time I interviewed the companies as much as they interviewed me. Although Kleiner Perkins was one of the companies I spoke with I decided to join another, newer venture capital firm, Rogers Schmidt. The Schmidt part is a guy I met at Stanford who was a year ahead of me in the MBA program. His dad is a big investment banker in San Francisco which helps.

My role with Rogers Schmidt is similar to what I was doing at Atari. I analyze companies, their product(s), team, and strategy. I'm a junior partner. That's relevant since there are only three senior partners, myself and one other junior partner. Plus I'm making 50% more than I made at Atari with a very lucrative bonus plan.

We invest in early stage, high growth potential, start-up companies. I try to quantify the risk which is something I love to do. The four companies we've funded since I started all have bright futures and we invest with an exit strategy of 3-5 years. We normally take an active role in the companies which includes seat(s) on their Board.

It seems there's always something going on up here. There are two new companies that incorporated this year that everyone is talking about, Apple with computers and Oracle for software. We weren't able to get into their capital raises but I might buy some of their stock if they become public.

Our office is in Menlo Park which is a very affluent area just north of Stanford. We're on Sand Hill Road which is the prime location for venture capital firms in the Valley. Both Maggie and I love the area and it's a good thing I'm making more money because housing is very expensive. Hopefully, my bonus this year will enable us to make a down payment on a home here. I'm also going to finish paying off my student loans by the end of this year. Yeah!

We're ready. Maggie and I are ready to start a family. She's been working for the Psychology Department at Cal and the nice part of her job is that she only has to be there twice a week. Whether she continues to work isn't really about the money, at least not now. It's more about what she wants to do. We're fortunate that I'm making enough money for us to live comfortably.

We had a scare in April when my dad had what the doctors are calling a minor heart attack. Luckily it happened on a weekend and my mom quickly called an ambulance. He was taken to the emergency room and spent two days in the hospital. Because of his family history of heart problems his doctor strongly advised him to start exercising and improve his diet. He's now on this new low fat Pritikin Diet. His problem was a wake-up call for me. I need to get more exercise and probably cut back on cocktails.

It's very refreshing to have Jimmy Carter as President and I love that he's pardoned Vietnam draft evaders. It's interesting that Ford pardoned Nixon but wouldn't pardon those who took a stand against that unjust war.

How about Led Zeppelin? After we heard about the attendance record they set in April at the Pontiac Silverdome just outside Detroit, something like 76,000, we really wanted to see them at the Oakland Alameda County Coliseum in July. Unfortunately we were in LA for one of Maggie's best girlfriend's wedding. Just as well we didn't go because I heard it was a bad scene when a fight between promoter Bill Graham's crew and the band's crew erupted. Besides, I've already seen Led Zeppelin at their absolute unforgettable best!

There's a phenomenon surrounding your image in my mind. Because I know almost nothing about you or if, in fact, you ever receive my letters I really don't need to think about things to ask you. That probably sounds strange but just reliving your image takes me to a wonderful place that needs nothing more.

Dan

August 9, 1978

Hi Tess,

The year started out great and Rogers Schmidt's growth has been remarkable.

After a year and a half I was welcomed as a senior partner, with a big raise and an even bigger bonus plan. We now employ a support staff of ten people and have helped fund a dozen companies. One of our first deals just paid off big time when the company was bought by the chip company Intel.

My bonus last year gave us the opportunity to buy a very small house in Menlo Park about a mile from my office. We bought the house from one of the original partners at Rogers Schmidt whose family had outgrown the two bedroom, one bath, single story home. I thought housing was expensive in parts of LA but it's ridiculously high here and it's only going up. We at least were able to avoid real estate commissions by handling the transaction privately.

We moved into the house in February and two weeks later found out Maggie was pregnant. The timing seemed perfect. Work was great, we had the house and now we were going to start our family. Then on a Wednesday morning I got a hysterical call from Maggie. She complained of bad abdominal pain and terrible cramps. I got home in a couple of minutes to find her rolled up in a fetal position on the bed. She had started to bleed so I wrapped her in a blanket and carried her to the car. In a few minutes were we at the hospital.

The news was devastating. Maggie had a miscarriage. The doctors thought she was probably in her 15th week. The physical pain Maggie incurred was nothing compared to the emotional scarring. I tried to do everything I could to help her but I wish I could have done more.

In discussions with her doctor, we were told they really don't know what causes miscarriages, and Maggie's family has no history of miscarriage. There are all sorts of causation theories but they're just theories. We got the best news we could hope for from the doctor when he gave Maggie a clean bill of health and his recommendation that we don't let the miscarriage affect our desire to have children.

I'd like to say the miscarriage didn't put a strain on our relationship, but it has. In hindsight, and after many months, I think I was too clinical. I relied too much on Maggie's male doctor whose role it is to be clinical. I thought if Maggie said she was okay she really was okay.

I wasn't good at reading her moods. Too often we search for simple answers when there are none.

We took our long awaited honeymoon in the middle of June and I hoped the change of scenery and beautiful beaches of Maui would rekindle our romance. It did, a little, for a while but wasn't a total cure. Unfortunately, I returned home to a ton of work that had accumulated over several months. I quickly resumed my normal 80 hour work week while Maggie spent most of her time at home, alone.

In July Maggie had the opportunity to get her old job at Cal back but declined. When I asked her what she wanted to do she'd just say she'd do something soon. I'm sure I didn't communicate my genuine concern properly but I get frustrated, too. Things seem better the last couple of weeks and hopefully we're past the first big stumbling block of our marriage. I think and hope I've learned a lot and I can't imagine my life without Maggie.

One night during our trip to Maui I tossed and turned unable to sleep. Trying to get back to sleep I tried to clear my mind and relax. Preoccupied with our relationship it was a welcome relief to see your image so bright and clear. And, for the first time I just wanted to hear your voice.

August 9, 1979

Dear Tess,

We had a baby girl! On July 8th Maggie gave birth to our precious bundle of joy, 8 lb Caroline Mae Brewster.

The best news is that both baby and mother are doing great. Maggie had a relatively easy pregnancy which was a huge relief after the miscarriage. I can't believe I'm a father and there's nothing better in the world than holding my beautiful daughter.

The miscarriage was the first real challenge of our relationship. We stumbled, fumbled and yet survived stronger than ever. I can just sit and watch Maggie and Caroline for hours. I don't know how people can tell Caroline looks like Maggie or me at a month old, but everyone seems to think she has my eyes.

Needless to say, Caroline's grandparents are overjoyed. She's the first grandchild for both our sets of parents. Maggie's mom, Susan, flew up a couple days before Caroline arrived and was a huge help. Maggie's dad, Rick, and my parents flew up the day after Caroline was born and stayed at a nearby hotel. They insisted on bringing in food for lunch and dinner the nights they were here. It was an amazing scene to watch six adults stare in wonderment at every movement and expression Caroline made. Luckily I took lots of movies.

Caroline arrived almost exactly on the predicted delivery date. To be safe we painted her room in a neutral light blue but her grandfathers insisted on adding a little pink trim to her room before they left. Her grandparents also made sure Caroline will be the best dressed baby in town.

With good reason Maggie was very worried about her pregnancy. She was meticulous about everything she ate and did. As her baby bump grew so did the glow on her face. We took Lamaze classes and I was in the delivery room to help Maggie with her breathing. Never did the miracle of life have more meaning. After seeing Maggie with Caroline I'm glad she wants to be a stay at home mom at least until Caroline starts school. Besides, my work is going great and I'm making more than enough money to support our family. Another year like the last and we'll be able to afford a bigger house. Remember, we want two kids.

Speaking of school, I now realize how important schools are when choosing where to live. We're blessed to be able to afford to live in an area of the country where education is emphasized above most everything else. A good friend of mine who has two kids has always told me, "When you have a child your life will never be the same." He was right.

Caroline was such a monumental event this year that it doesn't seem right to discuss other events that pale in comparison, but I do have one other comment. Tess, ten years ago today we saw Jethro Tull, Led Zeppelin, and each other. This is also the tenth letter I've sent you without knowing if you've received or read any of those letters. I can't explain why I think you have except to say I choose to believe it. Thank you for being with me these past ten years. Oh, there's one more thing. I'm constantly challenged by a grammar question. I always fumble with the words "affect" and "effect." I know the rule but I'm still a little confused. Sorry!

Dan

August 9, 1980

Dear Tess,

It's been another incredible year highlighted by our beautiful daughter.

Caroline weighs almost 20 lbs, can stand on her own, loves to put everything she can hold in her mouth and play with her toy phone. I think those are somewhat normal for a year old but she does do something that I'm sure is not normal. She likes to fall asleep to disco music, specifically music from Saturday Night Fever. I'm pretty much a rock guy but Maggie's a little more diverse and will listen to disco music when I'm not home. One afternoon she noticed Caroline had fallen asleep while Saturday Night Fever was playing on the stereo. The next day she purposely played the Saturday Night album when she put Caroline down for her afternoon nap. Bingo! Before the Bee Gees finished their first song, Stayin Alive, Caroline was asleep.

Certainly our little muffin gets more guests than her parents. One set or the other of her grandparents seems to visit every other week and there's a little two year old boy next door who likes to poke her belly and then giggle. Thank God, she's now sleeping through the night. The first few months were really rough especially on Maggie.

I've already got quite a collection of home movies and we're going to need an extra room to store all the clothes and toys she's outgrown. My favorite thing in the world is lying on my back on the couch and just watching her as she falls asleep on my chest.

Not only is Caroline great but so is business. The companies we're meeting with and investing in are predicting that in 10-20 years nearly every household in the country will have a personal computer. The stats we see today show less than 1% of households in the U.S. now have a personal computer. That means meteoric growth is going to produce some huge winners and Rogers Schmidt is positioned to take advantage of the tremendous opportunity. Unfortunately that also translates into long hours. Five years ago the 80 hour weeks didn't bother me as much. Today, I struggle with the guilt of missing too many of Caroline's "firsts."

Sometimes I feel like I'm living in the midst of a modern day Gold Rush. Sadly, the results aren't always positive. Too much money and too much overnight success can produce some unhappy endings. Gary, one of the guys in my networking group is living through that right now. His marriage has been destroyed because of at least two affairs he had that are now public. He frivolously blew through a lot of money on these women as his soon to be ex-wife sat at home with his three small children.

One night after our networking group get together he talked me into going out for a drink. I thought he wanted a friend to talk to or perhaps vent about the living hell he created. As we walked into the small hotel bar it seemed like the perfect place for a good conversation. There was only one other occupied table with two very attractive, very young gals dressed like they were going to a party in Vegas. I was shocked when one of the gals called out Gary's name. Next thing I know we're sitting at their table and Gary orders a bottle of expensive champagne.

It turns out Gary was having an affair with one of the gals. This wasn't going to be a coming to Jesus talk with Gary. These ladies wanted to party. I knew only trouble would come if I stayed. The problem was Gary had driven and my car was back at the office so I called a cab.

The girls were nice, too nice. Gary's friend was on his lap in minutes and the other gal was having fun reaching her hand into my pants pocket as she whispered in my ear, "What's that I feel in your pocket? It's getting bigger and harder. I'll bet it wants to come out and play. Let's find a more comfortable place and I'm sure I can help you with your problem."

Obviously, these weren't ordinary girls. I think the term is "escort." Luckily, my cab soon arrived. The temptation was very enticing, but I didn't even want to know her name. I didn't fall into the trap, said my goodbyes and in twenty minutes was home with my girls.

On the drive home I convinced myself I had nothing to hide. I did call a cab and came home as soon as I discovered what was happening. I walked into the house intending to tell Maggie everything, but she was sleeping and I didn't want to wake her.

Gary called me the next day at work to apologize. He was sorry for putting me in such a compromising situation, but was shocked when I told him I was going to tell Maggie what happened. He was relieved when I told him she was asleep when I got home. He couldn't believe any wife would believe the story. Maybe that's why he's getting a divorce. Surprisingly, at the end of our conversation he says, "She really liked you." I said the only thing I could, "Goodbye Gary."

Getting back to the business world, everything is great at Rogers Schmidt and because the housing market is so hot we're going to sell our house and buy a bigger three or four bedroom after the first of the year. We love where we're living and real estate up here is a great investment. Speaking of investments, word on the street is that Apple is about to IPO. (Go public) Once they do I'm going to buy 100 shares and put them in a special college fund for Caroline. College tuition keeps getting more expensive and we want to be sure she'll be able to pick her school assuming she gets good grades.

Caroline's parents are thinking she needs a brother or sister. We'd like to have our kids close in age and a bigger family is the reason for buying a larger home.

It looks like we're going to have an actor in the White House. With the Iran hostage crisis still looming and a declining economy, President Carter looks like easy pickings for our former governor, Ronald Reagan. I'm not nearly as political as I was in college and since most of my associates are conservative Republicans, concerned about taxes and government intervention in business, I keep my old liberal activism quiet.

Having the little one at home makes it difficult for us to go out but we did get a chance to see a great concert while Maggie's parents were visiting. We saw The Who at the Oakland Coliseum Arena in April. We hadn't seen them before and they were fantastic especially guitar-ist Pete Townsend. He does this big circular movement with his hand and arm. We loved Pinball Wizard, Won't Get Fooled Again and My Generation.

I hope I've been able to stay current on your address changes. My mailman keeps telling me if I haven't received the letters back then someone is receiving them. I hope that's you.

Dan

August 9, 1981

Hi Tess,

It's a good thing we bought a bigger house because we're having another baby!

Caroline is going to have a brother! Maggie's due in the middle of December and her pregnancy, so far, has been relatively smooth. The timing is perfect since the Valley pretty much shuts down between Thanksgiving and New Years and I'll be able to take most of December off.

Times sure have changed from my childhood. I don't remember the color of a baby's room being so important, but Maggie's been talking with her mother for weeks trying to decide on the right color combinations which of course affects the colors of all the baby accessories. After all, friends and family need to know those details to buy shower gifts.

Caroline is utterly amazing! She seems to do something for the first time almost every day. She still loves her disco and now dances to it. Strangely the other music she loves is Neil Young. Must be his raspy voice? I'll take credit for that since Neil is one of my all time favorites. She also seems to be curious about almost everything, especially when she can put it in her mouth. And she loves Dad to read to her, and that feeling is mutual. Last week I took a photo of her resting her head on Maggie's little baby bump. It's priceless.

Work continues to be an extremely rewarding challenge. Personal computers seem to be driving everything and Rogers Schmidt is investing heavily in some very exciting new software companies. I wonder if you have a computer and if you understand the difference between software and hardware. If not, here's a little help. Software is a program that performs a task on a computer and hardware is the device connected to the computer that allows the software to function. Hope that makes sense. We're investing in software companies because they're much more profitable than hardware companies. In fact, a software company we helped fund a year and a half ago was just acquired by Microsoft.

Well, Caroline got her college fund started off with 100 shares of Apple. They became a public company on Dec. 12th and created more millionaires, 300 (employees with stock or stock options and early investors) than any company in history. Word here on the street is that a couple of venture capitalists actually made hundreds of millions. Not that we need any more monetary incentive in our business but that's serious money.

A couple of months ago I took a tour of our dozen portfolio companies spending a couple of days at each. It was a wonderful experience to actually see how business is evolving. The offices are as different in décor as they are in employee dress. There still are the business types who wear a coat and tie but there's many more, primarily techies, who dress casual, and by casual I mean jeans, t-shirts and sneakers. When I see that it takes me back to Stanford and my brilliant nerd buddy Jeff. The tech guys also decorate their cubicles or office space with unique individuality. One of the electrical engineers decorated his office as a beach. I know that's probably hard to visualize but it was sort of cool. Bottom line, whatever makes these guys happy is good for business.

Surprisingly I've become good friends with my networking buddy Gary. We were reconnected because our firms are both involved in funding a new startup. His divorce was finally settled and he seems committed to his kids. He's a bright guy from a small town in Idaho who married his high school sweetheart when they were both nineteen. They had three children in rapid succession, before Gary and his wife, Cheryl, were 24. Nineteen is awful young to get married and certainly their marriage would have had a better chance if they still lived in their small Idaho hometown. Instead, Gary found himself in Silicon Valley and the middle of the tech explosion. When you understand his story you can see how his life unraveled.

Not surprisingly the two women he had affairs with are long gone. He accepts responsibility for his destructive behavior and has become sort of a spokesman for the evils of "too much, too soon." Also, it helps that Maggie really likes him. Guess you can call him my best friend in the Valley.

Although Maggie and I like to get down to LA whenever we can it's been difficult lately with Caroline and the baby to be. Our spare bedrooms are getting plenty of use. Between our families and friends we seem to have very welcome guests almost every weekend. Maggie loves to entertain, much more than me. My specialty is firing up the barbecue.

Even though I'm a Democrat I have to give President Reagan credit for negotiating the release of the hostages held in Iran for fourteen months. Also, I like that he put the first woman, Sandra Day O'Connor, on the Supreme Court. His big test is still what he does to control our 10% inflation and terribly high interest rates.

Tess, I hope life finds you happy and healthy. I regularly ask the mailman who delivers to our office if the rules for forwarding mail are the same. I choose to believe you are still receiving my letters just as I choose to believe what happened to us in Anaheim twelve years ago was not an accident.

Dan

August 9, 1982

Hi Tess,

On the morning of December 14th we welcomed Benjamin Sullivan Brewster to the world and our family.

His arrival came off without a hitch and as with Caroline I was in the delivery room trying to help Maggie. This time I knew what to expect. As with Caroline, Maggie's parents came up to help out and this time we had a guest room for them.

I'm so excited to have a son. I absolutely adore my wonderful daughter but a son has just been a different experience for me. I can't wait to teach him how to build things or how to ride a bike or throw a baseball. I'm so, so lucky to have such a beautiful family.

There is nothing sweeter than watching Caroline with her baby brother and I've tried to capture everything on film. Ben seems to be a lot different than his sister was. He's quieter, not as animated and much more serious. Now that we have two children I can't imagine my world without them. Nothing in my life can compare to being a Father.

Business is going crazy. It seems like there's another new company started almost every day. We've been looking into two, Sun Microsystems and Symantec. Sun was founded by three former Stanford students and is building a workstation combining a Unix Operating System and Motorola processors. Symantec is working on all sorts of artificial intelligence technology including databases. Those descriptions of what they do are directly from their Company materials and I'm glad you can't ask me to explain them further. Obviously I need to do more homework.

The latest "hot new technology" seems to be networking. Instead of connecting people we're talking about connecting computers. At the end of June we heard a brilliant engineer at a Stanford conference talk about how one day everyone will be connected and eventually without any wires. I spoke with this engineer after his presentation and he's scheduled to give a presentation at our office in September. What he talks about could be a game changer or as we call it up here a "paradigm shift."

Sometimes I have to pinch myself to believe how much money I'm making. I guess it's about being in the right place at the right time. Also, the best decision I've ever made, besides marrying Maggie, was to get my MBA from Stanford. The connections and relationships I made at Stanford have opened and continue to open doors.

Tess, I seem to be able to tell you things I can't tell anyone else which becomes an even more bewildering thought since I still can't explain our relationship. I don't think intimacy can be one sided, can it?

That last paragraph was a prelude to what I'm about to write. Maggie and I seem to have grown apart after the birth of Ben, much like we did after Caroline was born. I've done a little research and think it's called postpartum depression. Normally Maggie is the sweetest most even tempered person I know. She usually has more energy than me, including sexual energy. She's the wild child. Since Ben was born that's all changed. She's irritable, has irrational mood swings, no interest in sex and always seems to be tired. We've talked to our doctor who told us it's not unusual for a woman to experience this after childbirth. I try to be patient and understanding because I know this is not my Maggie, but sometimes when I try to be sympathetic and helpful she'll just snap at me and I withdraw to my cave and another glass of scotch. Hopefully this will pass soon.

On a brighter note we're giving both sets of parents a special Christmas gift this year, an all expense paid trip to Hawaii. They can go anytime after the first of the year. All they have to do is tell us when and what island(s) and we'll make all the arrangements. Although our parents are good friends they'll probably go separately since my folks like to hang out on the beach while Maggie's parents golf and shop. They've done so much for both of us and their grandkids we want to do something special for them.

The rise of business here in the Valley is in direct contrast to most of the country which is dealing with a recession. High unemployment, high interest rates and high inflation are a terrible threesome and I keep waiting for things to turn around. I'm afraid we're going to have a lot more bank failures thanks to the recession and deregulation of the banking system. I heard a stat that was indicative of the problem we face when a Savings and Loan can leverage $2 million into $1.3 billion in loans. Unbelievable!

I hope all my talk about business doesn't bore you but it's the world in which I live. As always, wish you the best.

Dan

August 9, 1983

Dear Tess,

It's been an extremely difficult year for Maggie and me. First, we tragically discovered our little Ben has autism. Then I did the unthinkable and had an affair that threatened our marriage.

Soon after Ben was born we noticed rather obvious differences in behavior between him and Caroline at the same age. We assumed boys were just different as are all children. We didn't think it was anything abnormal. Then the different signs kept escalating and Ben's behavior began to worry us. Sadly, the word "no" became the word we had to insert in front of his behavior: no big smiles, no facial expressions and no gestures. He also rarely made eye contact, didn't respond to his name or our voices, and didn't make noise to get our attention.

We initially addressed the problems with Ben's pediatrician who, at first, didn't think the issues were abnormal or would be permanent. Several months later, when things became worse we again visited our pediatrician. This time Dr. Steinlen referred us to a specialist, Dr. Winston Miller who ran an exhaustive series of tests on Ben.

I'll never forget Dr. Miller's words after examining Ben. "It appears to be autism. Unfortunately, there is no cure at the present time." Maggie and I were devastated.

We sought a second opinion and drove to LA to meet with one of the world's foremost experts at the UCLA Medical Center, Dr. Ruth Weisman. Unfortunately her diagnosis was the same as Dr. Miller's. Dr. Weisman also shared more information. Autism is reported in about 1 in 10,000 children although that number may be deceiving since many parents probably never have the behavioral problems of their children properly diagnosed. Autism also has a 3:1 ratio of boys over girls and it wasn't until the last few years that autism was classified as a developmental disorder.

Unbelievably, in the 60's and 70's treatment was all over the map and even included hallucinogens such as LSD, electric shock, and even pain and punishment. Thank God this is 1983 and autism is now treated with behavioral therapy and the integration of highly controlled learning environments. Dr. Weisman referred us to a colleague closer to home at the University of California San Francisco.

I've never felt worse about anything and it certainly changed my perspective on what's really important in life. There is no escaping the reality that our precious son has a behavioral disorder for which there's no cure.

This horrific situation also put a big crack in my relationship with Maggie. We became more and more distant, much worse than what we experienced during her postpartum depression. To escape reality I started to drink, more and more. While I like a drink to relax when I get home it increased to a couple of drinks, then three and even four. I drank to escape the pain but all it did was cause greater pain.

My behavior turned from self-destruction to the possible destruction of my marriage and family when one evening I stopped at a local bar to have a drink before going home. I spotted a very attractive woman who looked familiar, but I couldn't place her face. As I looked over at her, she smiled and then it dawned on me. She was the gal I met with Gary over three years ago who playfully put her hand in my front pants pocket. Only this night I wasn't anxious to get home.

When I approached her table she greeted me with, "I remember you. You're Gary's friend. It's been a long time." I ordered her another Cosmo and myself another scotch.

I was shocked to find her very bright and also very forthright. She had gone back to college at San Jose State and was of all things, a business major. She enjoyed bright men who would pay her directly for her company. She claimed to be very selective because she could afford to be. She promised there would never be any complications, only a discreet rendezvous. Her time was not cheap and neither was she. She claimed her name really was Hope.

Twenty minutes later we were having wild sex in a nearby hotel. Probably twenty-five years old, she was not only beautiful but also very fit. It had been more than fourteen years since I had been with a woman other than Maggie. Hell, I've only had sex with three women in my life. In thirty minutes we were finished. At the time I rationalized it was an adventure and another way for me to escape all the pain. I gave her $600 for her time and another $50 for cab fare. She gave me her number and I left her with a hug.

My mood changed 180° before I even got into my car. The guilt was overwhelming. I felt like shit. What the hell had I done? Was I going crazy? I sat in my car for ten minutes, trembling and crying. I've never been more ashamed of anything in my life. I didn't know what to do? Maggie knows me so well and usually notices everything. Do I tell her what happened, or keep my mouth shut? I had absolutely no possible justification or explanation. Once I started my car I wished the drive home was five hours instead of five minutes. Before I got home I cowardly decided to keep quiet and see a shrink or therapist.

Thank God Maggie was asleep when I got home and I couldn't wait to take a shower. I didn't sleep that night replaying the sordid evening over and over again. In the morning I lied to Maggie about where I was and quickly left for the office hoping my abrupt behavior didn't raise any red flags.

First thing I did once I got to the office was call my friend Gary. I asked him to meet me for lunch. I had Gary swear he'd keep what I was about to tell him absolutely confidential. He was the one person I knew who could relate and he did. He gave me the name of the therapist who had helped him and suggested I didn't wait as long as he did to see him.

Back in the office I closed my office door, something I rarely do and called the therapist to set up an appointment. That was three months ago, and although I continue in therapy, I still haven't told Maggie. Unfortunately, the situation at home hasn't changed. My therapist keeps insisting I bring Maggie with me but I haven't had the courage to do it.

Tess, for the first time in my life I'm lost and riddled with guilt I can't escape. I apologize for venting all this on you and sharing my despicable behavior but for whatever reason I feel like I can tell you anything.

Dan

August 9, 1984

Dear Tess,

Things are better now but not before I went through a self-caused hell.

I'm blessed Maggie is the most wonderful, most forgiving partner in the world. She's much more than I deserve. We finally went to therapy together and unbelievably she took responsibility for much of my behavior. I still can't believe she would do that. She said her postpartum depression drove us apart and Ben's autism added even more stress to our relationship.

Part of therapy was an agreement I made with myself and Maggie. I finally came to terms with my drinking problem and agreed to limit myself to one drink a day. If I couldn't do that I agreed to totally stop drinking and go to Alcoholics Anonymous. Maggie and I still go to therapy twice a month to discuss our issues and resolve them before they escalate. As a result of the therapy we're communicating much, much better.

I've also stopped drinking except for maybe a glass of red wine at dinner. I really don't miss it and realize my drinking is directly related to my stress level.

I can't believe Caroline is five. She continues to be a truly amazing, gifted child and is getting ready to start kindergarten. Sometimes I think her favorite words are why and how. Her vocabulary is probably better than mine and she reads more than Maggie and I combined. Her favorite game while we're driving is to solve math problems in her head. Her most endearing quality is how she protects her brother and the patience she has with him. There's no question she's Maggie's daughter.

My precious son Ben will be three in December and remains both my biggest responsibility and concern in life. He seems to respond best to Caroline while he's aloof to most other children. His world is just not social and speech is difficult. Maggie takes him for individual therapy once a week and to a special class for autistic preschoolers twice a week. I've made it a priority to stay on top of all the research and studies being done and hope one day there will be a cure. Maggie and I established a special fund to insure he will always have the means to be taken care of if anything should happen to us. Ironically, Ben has taught me more about life than anyone. One day I hope to share so much with my son.

My life is simple compared to Maggie's who is continually dropping off or picking up one of the kids. I take a lot more work home so I can help her out and we also hired Sarah, a very sweet 65 year old grandmother of six, who comes to the house three days a week to help Maggie.

Work has been busy, as usual. One of our early investments paid off big, meaning our original investment of $1 million returned $20 million in two years. That's not the norm but when it happens it's very rewarding in many ways. Technology that connects people still seems the future and that's our focus at Rogers Schmidt.

I attended a fascinating presentation last month by an author of a book called The Reasons for Silicon Valley Success. It emphasized the significance of the young creative minds here that were influenced by the anti-establishment, alternative lifestyle of the late 60's and 70's. The Valley became fun and ideals vs. East Coast money and status and the Valley's three pronged motto became: question authority, think differently and change the world.

Our lives have certainly changed since Maggie and I moved here. Our life is now about family and we're very blessed, even with the challenges we've faced along the way. I wake up every morning hoping to read about a cure for autism. One day it will happen.

Dan

August 9, 1985

Tess,

After several tumultuous years, this past year was a welcome relief.

Maggie and I have reconnected and our communication is much, much better. I've made a concerted effort to improve my behavior including working less and helping more with Caroline and Ben. I've also lived up to my agreement to control my drinking. No more scotch for me. No more stopping for a drink before I go home and the only woman in my life is Maggie.

Although it's been a work in progress Maggie and I have regained our intimacy. Finding time for sex is a challenge with two young kids but we try to be creative time wise and once every three or four months a set of grandparents fly up to stay with the kids while Maggie and I take a weekend vacation. Last year we went to Vegas, Santa Barbara and Palm Springs. The trips recharge our batteries and give us important alone time.

The kids both seemed to have a good year. Actually, Caroline had a remarkable year. She really is a gifted child and her 1st grade teacher thinks she's at a third grade level and can probably skip a grade without any problems. The public schools are excellent here but we're exploring whether she would have more opportunities at a private school.

Ben's behavior has stabilized and we keep trying to be the best parents we can. He's becoming more affectionate which we love. He's still very shy with others, except for his relationship with Caroline. Remarkably, she seems to understand Ben better than anyone. Most of the time he seems to be in his own world and it's difficult for him to show emotions. Maggie still takes him to therapy once a week and a special preschool twice a week. We're exploring all the schools in the area that have programs for autistic children.

Business never gets boring. We're looking at investing in another couple of companies that make mobile phone components. Currently there are roughly 300,000 mobile phone users in the US. The forecasts we see estimate that number will grow to five million in 1990 and then 100 million by 2,000. If those projections are true there's going to be some big winners and we're trying to identify those companies now.

Rogers Schmidt continues to grow our investment portfolio and I'm now serving as a director on the boards of three companies we've helped fund. The excitement of the technology we see and the enthusiasm of the bright people that present their companies is another wonderful reason I love working at Rogers Schmidt. Because almost all the partners have families with young children there's an added commonality we all share. We all understand the demands of being a parent and trying to balance work and family.

Less than a month ago we were treated to what might have been the greatest rock concert of all time, Live Aid, sorry Woodstock devotees. It would have been great to attend the actual concerts in London or Philly but the TV coverage was excellent and I understand it was watched by a billion people globally. Live Aid certainly had the best lineup ever. Who would have ever thought we'd get to see Elton John, Madonna, Santana, Sting, the Beach Boys, Queen, U2, Tom Petty, Eric Clapton and my favorite, Neil Young, all performing on the same day. Making the day even more memorable was the fact it raised over $100 million for famine relief in Africa.

One of the reasons I love living in this area is the consciousness level. A couple weeks ago, Maggie and I and another couple drove to Berkeley to hear a symposium on AIDS or acquired immune deficiency syndrome. Not sure how big this is in the rest of the country but there's more and more news about it up hear every week. The auditorium was packed and the speakers addressed the latest research. There is consensus that AIDS is caused by a virus that attacks our blood. About seventy percent of those with AIDS are either homosexual or bisexual and almost 20% of the victims are intravenous drug users. Predictions were ominous including a full blown epidemic. It's estimated AIDS has affected 8,000+ in the US with more than 4,000 deaths. San Francisco, driven by it high proportion of homosexuals, is driving public awareness. Hopefully treatment and a cure will come soon.

Tess, please be well and happy.

Dan

August 9, 1986

Hi Tess,

I wish I could always start with good news but I guess that's not life.

In February, my mother, Laura found out she had breast cancer. Luckily her doctor discovered it early during her annual physical. A biopsy indicated the small lump was malignant and after consulting with several doctors she had a lumpectomy which is a procedure where only the tumor and surrounding tissue is removed. The surgery only took about 30 minutes and since it was done with a local anesthetic mom came home later the same day.

I flew down the day of the surgery to be with my mom. She is an incredibly strong woman. I hadn't realized her family has a history of breast cancer which is important because heredity influences can indicate a propensity for cancer. My parents, with the exception of my dad's minor heart attack years ago have been very healthy. My father, Carl, is now sixty while mom is fifty-eight. Everything always comes back to our health.

Our precocious daughter, Caroline, is now going to a special school for gifted and high achieving children. Switching schools was a difficult decision but was made easier when one of her best girlfriends, whose parents are both teachers, decided to send their daughter there. Along with the change in schools Caroline also advanced a full year. She seems to be flourishing and continues to keep me on my toes with questions that keep getting harder to answer. My most frequent response is, "Better ask your Mother."

Ben is growing up quickly and will be five in December. Every so often he'll surprise us by doing something new and it gives us hope for his future. Maggie has unbelievable patience and understanding with him but it takes its toll on her. Too often, I'll wake up in the middle of the night to hear her sobbing in bed. Coping is an everyday challenge but Maggie and I are committed to making Ben's life as complete and happy as possible.

I'm continually amazed at the companies that present their business plans to Rogers Schmidt. A case in point is a company we saw in the spring. There was an event that occurred in January when the first computer virus called "brain" was released, by accident, and infected and disabled computers around the world. The presentation we saw was in response to the threat of the computer virus. The company saw this as a staggering problem going forward and is close to developing security programs that will rid computers of a virus. If they're right about this being a significant problem, the solution could be huge.

There really shouldn't be much of a difference between being thirty-four and thirty-five but for some reason I feel more middle aged— now. I keep saying I need to get back to the gym but there doesn't seem to be enough time in the day. I've bought some crazy exercise equipment off TV but after trying them once they end up in a corner of the garage. The days of playing hoops with the guys are over so I'm going to start running and try to get back in shape. I'll have to run early in the morning but I need to do it.

We took our first family road trip in July. We rented a motor home and drove to Yosemite and Lake Tahoe. We thought it would be easier to drive than fly. It's just so damn hard to know what's going on with Ben. I want so much to be able to do so many simple fun things with him. It just sucks. I try to be strong but there are times I'm just overwhelmed and breakdown in tears. Perhaps that's what makes thirty-five so difficult. Sorry for the tone of this letter but, as always, hope you're well and prospering.

Dan

August 9, 1987

Hi Tess,

I hope you remember my old Stanford friend, Jeff, the nerd genius. He worked at the Palo Alto Research Center, a division of Xerox until last year when he decided to start his own company. Now he's invented a new way to speed up the connectivity between computers and he recently gave a presentation at our office. The technology had most of us baffled but our resident techie at Rogers Schmidt thinks it's brilliant.

At our partner meeting I was the primary advocate for investing in Jeff's three man firm, but first we had to get a legal opinion from our attorneys and make sure there would be no claims from Xerox that the technology was developed while Jeff was employed by them. Our law firm interviewed Jeff, reviewed all his paperwork and concluded there was no conflict. That's the okay we needed and Rogers Schmidt agreed to invest $1.2 million in Jeff's company paid in three equal amounts upon the completion of specified milestones. Because of my relationship with Jeff I'm more excited about this deal than any other we've ever done at the firm.

It's always so easy to write about Caroline but always much more difficult to write about Ben. This past year Maggie and I made a conscious effort to get much more proactive in dealing with the challenges of autism. First, we're going weekly to a parent's autism awareness group organized by Ben's school. At the meetings, run by a psychologist, parents share their experience and challenges in raising an autistic child. It's very helpful to know how other parents cope with their kids and there's a bonding that takes place between parents who can relate with what others are going through. We also learn what works and what doesn't work for other parents.

The second action we've taken is to get involved with a local autism charity. Besides our financial donation Maggie had been chosen to be on their board. The mission of the charity is to increase the awareness of autism and raise money for autism research that will hopefully lead to successful treatment and eventually a cure. We've also met some wonderful people who have become good friends.

Our involvement with the parents group and the charity have substantially increased our knowledge of autism and also taught us that autism is a moving target in several ways. First, children's behavior can change over time, even to the point of normalcy. Secondly, research is changing acceptable treatment. No one would think of giving a child LSD, electric shock or other painful treatment as they did in the 60's. Indeed, anyone who would, should be arrested.

Prescribed medication is currently a very controversial subject and much more research needs to be conducted before any specific medication is widely accepted. The problem is complicated because valid testing takes a long time and considerable expense. With new drugs being invented all the time the standards for testing create a slippery slope, especially if you're a parent with an autistic child who wants so desperately to help their child. As I reread this paragraph it accurately reflects the complexity and confusion of addressing what to do as a parent of an autistic child.

Like autism itself, Ben's behavior is a moving target subject to rapid change. We believe his therapy and special classes have helped his learning challenges and definitely have lessened his depression. He also seems to be much more comfortable with the familiar faces at school. We only hope to keep moving forward.

Caroline continues to be an absolute joy. Maggie and I agree her intelligence is far above where we were at her age and that's been confirmed by both sets of our parents. Besides her smarts she is such a sweet caring little girl who just melts her dad's heart. I've captured some remarkable movies of her interacting with Ben that's priceless and guaranteed to bring tears to your eyes.

The good news is that everyone in our families had a healthy year. I've even started to run. It means I get up at five and run mostly in the dark but it's been very worthwhile. Besides losing 10 lbs I feel and sleep better. On weekends I run with a neighbor who's trying to talk me into running a 10k. We'll see.

Tess, writing a letter on the same date each year to the same person with whom I have such a unique relationship reads like a book or a movie. I continue to believe you're receiving and reading my letters. Thank you for your silent voice and all you represent.

Dan

August 9, 1988

Hi Tess,

We have recently become a musical family. Caroline asked for and received a guitar for her ninth birthday on July 8. Now, only a month later she's trying to play the Neil Young songs she already sings. As much as I love his music I'm not sure it's the best choice for a nine year old girl.

The day after Caroline's birthday Ben tried to play her guitar like a drum. So, we did the obvious and bought a small drum set for our son. He loves to bang on them and I think it's almost therapeutic for him. I wish I could say the same for my ears.

In December we took our first long distance family vacation and flew to Disney World. We stayed at the Disney Polynesian Resort and had a great time. Having been to Disneyland a half dozen times I couldn't believe how big Disney World was. It sure makes Disneyland seem small. Most importantly, Ben seemed to enjoy himself and any worry we had for him on the plane was unjustified. It was really a lot of fun traveling as a family and of course I've got photographs to prove it.

Maggie and I are both getting more and more involved in the search to find effective treatment and a cure for autism. I was told by a researcher that the number of reported cases keeps growing and a wide range of potential causation factors are being investigated including environmental toxins such as mercury contained in air pollution, pesticides and vaccines. The cause of autism remains a baffling mystery.

One spring afternoon I left work early to pick Caroline up from school. After I gave her a big kiss she asked me, "Daddy can I have an Apple?" My response seemed logical, "Sure, wait till we get home and you can have all the apples you want." "No Daddy, not that kind of Apple, I want an Apple computer, a Macintosh." I almost hit a parked car.

Apparently one of the kids at her school has an Apple computer. That makes sense since I think her friend's dad works for Apple. I told Caroline I had a surprise for her at home, but before she got too excited I had to tell her it wasn't a computer. Once we got home I told her to sit in the kitchen and have an apple while I got her surprise. I then went to the desk in our bedroom and pulled out my Charles Schwab statements to show her the Apple stock she owns. What followed was a simple lesson on the stock market, stock ownership and investing. From that day forward, Caroline makes it a habit to check the share price of Apple at least once a week. To make the story complete, Caroline got her Apple computer for her ninth birthday and her dad just loves her Apple story. (It would make a great Apple commercial)

My running has escalated and I ran my first race, not a 10k, but the famous Bay to Breakers.(12k) The race starts a few blocks from the Embarcadero on San Francisco Bay and meanders west through the city to the ocean. What an unbelievable experience. There were 100,000 participants and people were dressed in the wildest costumes imaginable including all sorts of strung together insects, naked or partially naked exhibitionists and probably 500 costumed Elvis impersonators. It's pretty much a big moving party.

Time has become the limiting resource for Maggie and me. We need more and because we do scheduling is critical. Caroline seems to have something going on every day after school and on weekends and we're always taking or picking up Ben from school or therapy. The reality is that Maggie works harder than I do.

Speaking of work, our percentage of hits and home runs at Rogers Schmidt is running at about 40% which is extremely high for venture capital firms. Fortunately pulling the plug financially or watching an unsuccessful company fail is tempered by the reality in the Valley that failure often produces some of the biggest successes.

Tess, your image pops up in my head often. Sometimes I'll be at a ballgame or a restaurant and see a woman whose blonde hair looks like you from behind.

August 9th

When that happens, I always wait intently for her to turn around. If only life was that simple.

Dan

August 9, 1989

Dear Tess,

Twenty years ago today we attended a landmark rock concert in Anaheim featuring two relatively new bands, Jethro Tull and Led Zeppelin.

So much has happened in the world, the United States and our own lives since that day. Yet, throughout those past twenty years the image of you briefly turning around twice at that the end of the concert remains a treasured memory in my life. Time has passed but your vivid image fueled through my eyes, processed in my head and captured in my heart is as powerful as it was on August 9, 1969.

Instead of looking back one year I now have the luxury of looking back over the last twenty. Maggie has been the most important part of those years. She has been my rock, my light and often my conscience. She has tolerated me when I couldn't tolerate myself and she believed in me when I lost my way. I loved her madly twenty years ago and I love her even more today.

Children change your life forever, but it's the best change one can ever experience. Although we think its parents who teach children I've learned more from Caroline and Ben than any two people in the world. Caroline has been easy from day one while Ben has been and continues to be a challenge. But, both are absolute joys and I can't love anyone more than I love them. There is no more challenging job than parenting and although I have learned much there is still more that I strive to become. I love being Maggie's husband but I am proudest of being Caroline and Ben's father.

Work has been much more than I ever expected. To be in probably the most exciting work environment in the world is a dream come true. I get paid handsomely to meet some of the most brilliant people on the planet, hear their plans for making life easier, faster and more rewarding and then help them achieve those goals. I love my job and certainly appreciate the financial rewards that translate into greater freedom and opportunity for my family.

Today, I savor the past and look forward to every minute of the future. I can't wait to watch Caroline and Ben grow and I will do all in my power to make sure my son has every opportunity and all the blessings he so deserves in life.

Tess, it's been a wild and rewarding twenty years. I continue to wish you good health, happiness and limitless opportunity.

Dan

August 9, 1990

Dear Tess,

It was a wonderful year highlighted by two family trips.

In December we drove to Squaw Valley for our first family winter vacation. Neither Maggie nor I had skied since college and it showed. Caroline had never been on skis yet was skiing circles around us by the time we left. Ben seemed to enjoy it, too.

A friend from our parental autism group referred us to Carol, a special ski instructor who works with autistic children in the Bay area during the off-season. Finding Carol was a big help and she's married to Steve, another ski instructor. We hired them both for two hours each morning. We'd all go up the mountain together and then either Maggie or I would ski with Ben or Caroline and one of the instructors. Finally, Maggie and I are past our trepidation of going places and doing things with Ben. It's been our issue, not his and he deserves the opportunity to experience life.

In June we took a very different trip to Washington DC. Caroline had done so much research on her Apple before we left she had our itinerary all worked out. It was the perfect time for her to have the ultimate US history lesson. We stayed at a hotel near the White House and Capitol and loved being able to walk everywhere. It's always difficult trying to figure out what's going on in Ben's head but I think he enjoyed the trip.

Caroline continues to amaze us. She recited most of the Gettysburg Address as we stood looking up at the marvelous Lincoln Memorial. She also named all the Supreme Court Justices while Maggie and I combined could only name six.

For me, the highlight of the trip was around the corner from the Lincoln Memorial. It was the Vietnam Veterans Memorial and specifically the Memorial Wall inscribed with all our servicemen who lost their lives in that war. Since I opposed that war so aggressively I initially had a very difficult time looking at the wall. Then, for the first time in my life I came to terms with the reality that those 58,000 troops who gave their lives were the forgotten victims of our corrupt leaders. Teary eyed I also searched, found and touched my high school friend's name on the wall.

We've decided to move again and have put our house up for sale. There are four new homes being built on a cul-de-sac a couple of miles from us and we're looking into buying one of these five bedroom six bath two story houses. Rogers Schmidt continues to be more and more successful and the partner's yearly bonus is well into seven figures. It sure makes those 80 hour work weeks seem worthwhile.

Caroline seems to excel in almost everything she does. The exception would be her singing. Luckily she realized this early on and while her guitar sits in her closet she's out riding her horse, Ernie, or in a gymnastics class. I don't know how she finds the time to help her dad on the computer.

Can you believe Ben will turn nine in December? It seems like Applied Behavioral Analysis (ABA) is the preferred method of treatment today even though it was originally developed in the 60's. The focus is on teaching motor, social and reasoning skills with positive reinforcement when the child shows the correct behavior. Ben receives one-on-one treatment from a teacher at his school who has tailored a program specifically for him. She also tries to discover what triggers his unwanted behavior.

Maggie continues to be very active in fund raising for the autism charity and has become somewhat an expert on the disorder. I don't know how she finds time but she does. Luckily Sarah is still with us and she's been a fantastic help. The kids just adore her and Ben has really bonded with her over time. I'm not sure if I mentioned that Sarah has grandchildren, but she's got six. She was thrown into being a single mom in Oakland at the age of twenty-five when her husband just left one day never to return. She worked six days a week cleaning houses to support her family but still found time to raise a beautiful son and daughter who both graduated from college.

Sarah really has become part of our family and makes our lives so much easier. We've had a minivan for a couple of years and for last Christmas we surprised Sarah and her family with their own brand new Dodge minivan. We invited her two children, their spouses and all her grandchildren out for dinner and gave her keys to the minivan which was in the parking lot adjacent to the restaurant. She certainly deserves it.

Actually, the idea to buy Sarah a minivan was not mine. I suggested we send her on a trip to Hawaii (My usual gift suggestion) but was overruled by the coalition of Maggie and Caroline. When I told them I thought the van idea was a little extravagant Maggie quickly replied, "What's extravagant is the amount of money you make." This was the first time I felt the collective weight of girl power in my family and I'm afraid it's a force I can't overcome.

Unfortunately I've had to stop running because of an injury, plantar fasciitis, which is caused by straining the ligament that supports your arch. It's my left foot and the only way for it to heal is to stop running. Interestingly, I'm still up by 5:00.

All-in-all it's been a very good year. I hope yours has been the same.

August 9, 1991

Tess,

It finally happened. I turned forty in February.

I remember when that seemed so old and so far away. Today, I don't feel very different than I did at twenty-five although Maggie takes joy in pulling out what she claims are grey hairs from the back of my head. One of the guys at the office insists forty is the new thirty and I'll buy that.

We sold our house in about two weeks for 50% more than we paid for it and bought our new dream home to replace our last dream home. This 8,000 sq. ft. brand new two story has 5 bedrooms, 6 baths, 3 fireplaces and my favorite, a pizza oven. I think furnishing the house cost almost as much as our first house. I've given up trying to understand why most of the perfectly good furniture from our old house doesn't work in our new house. The good news is that we're in the same neighborhood and that makes everything easier for all of us.

August 9th

It's been a challenging year. Poor Ben had a couple of incidents. The first was a meltdown while we were out to dinner. We don't know what set him off but I had to carry him to the safety of our car and just hold him for twenty minutes until he settled down. The second problem came at school when he took a swing at another boy. This was particularly significant because, with rare exception, he hasn't displayed aggressive behavior.

Because of these two incidents Maggie and I now keep a diary of Ben's daily behavior trying to find reasons for how he acts. We include what he eats, how he sleeps, who he interacts with and anything out of the ordinary. We're also trying to be hyperaware of cues he may be giving us that are reflective of something he's trying to tell us believing there is a reason for everything. He'll be ten in December and keeps getting bigger and stronger. His safety, and the safety of those around him, is always our number one concern. It's beyond frustrating to love someone so much and not be able to help him, but Maggie and I will never stop trying.

On the other end of the spectrum, Caroline continues to be a wonder child. Now twelve, she wears me out intellectually and I struggle with some of the problems and assignments she brings home from school. Without her knowing it, Maggie and I got duplicate copies of her text books so we could review what she's going to be studying before we get her barrage of questions. Her favorite question continues to always start with "why." Her mind is like a sponge and she never seems to forget anything.

Ben and Caroline challenge us constantly and Maggie and I are mentally exhausted by the end of the day. This has put a strain on our sex life and we've tried to set up date nights at least once every couple of weeks but most of the time something always seems to come up and we have to cancel on ourselves.

Rogers Schmidt continues to gain momentum as one of the top venture capital firms in the Valley. The innovative technology that comes through our office is never ending and the individuals behind the ideas keep getting younger and younger. At one time being a graduate from Harvard or Stanford or MIT seemed to be the recipe for success. Now it seems being a dropout from one of those institutions can be even more significant, the best examples being co-founders Steve Jobs and Steve Wozniak of Apple and Bill Gates and Paul Allen of Microsoft.

We had my parents up here last month and I'm concerned about my dad. He worked his whole life to be able to retire and now that he has he's bored to death. I can't figure out what the hell he does all day long but he says he stays busy. Meanwhile he's put on more weight and his idea of exercise is walking to the mailbox to pick up his social security and retirement checks. I'm trying to get him involved in something he enjoys rather than just watching sports on television. The lesson I've learned is retirement is overrated and probably outdated.

Maggie and I did see a great concert recently. Our family flew down to LA and after we left Caroline and Ben in the welcome arms of Maggie's parents, we saw

Guns N' Roses at the Forum. Haven't seen this much energy from a band in a long time and they played more than thirty songs including their anthems Welcome to the Jungle, Sweet Child of Mine and Paradise City. Axl Rose always reminds me of Jim Morrison.

Tess, I had the craziest dream a couple of months ago that found you in my all time favorite Neil Young song, Cowgirl in the Sand. I saw you from behind while you were horseback riding on the beach in Maui. I kept trying to catch up to you and called out, "Tess, Tess!" Just when you started to turn around I woke up. Is that our fate or is it all just a dream?

Dan

August 9, 1992

Dear Tess,

This is a letter I almost didn't write because of my disgust with myself and the guilt that consumes me. My despicable behavior and character flaws once again have threatened my soul and those I love most. Somehow I've lost whatever conscience I had.

My self caused living hell isn't over. I'm in the midst of trying to find the courage to confess to the only woman I've ever loved and can't live without. Three days ago I ended the free fall that's caused my problem but I haven't had the balls to tell anyone, not even my friend Gary or my therapist. For a reason I'm beginning to understand, I feel like I can tell you anything and everything.

It wasn't planned. It all started very innocently and unexpectedly. Rogers Schmidt was considering an investment in a start-up software company in June. As is typical, the company founders gave their presentation in our office and I then made an appointment to spend a couple days in their office talking with their staff and checking out what they're doing firsthand. That's what I do, analyze and make a recommendation.

After spending a couple of hours with the two founders I was given a tour of their small offices and then introduced individually to their handful of employees. As with most start-ups, almost everyone has an impressive title since it's much easier to hand out titles than money. Except for the small corner office the founders shared, the remaining office space was divided into cubicles. When I was introduced to their VP of marketing I was shocked. Trying not to look like I'd just seen a ghost I shook hands with the very attractive woman. It was a handshake that felt like foreplay as she squeezed my hand then let go of her grip only to squeeze my hand even harder.

There stood Hope, probably the last woman in the world I wanted to see. Nine years after we had one night of drunken sex that nearly destroyed me and my marriage here she was, but now she was working for a start-up Rogers Schmidt was evaluating for a possible investment.

As I listened to the CEO praise Hope Bennett and her marketing plan, I flashed back nine years and Hope telling me she was only an escort to pay her way through college. Back then she was going to San Jose State. I also remembered how she stroked my ego by telling me she really liked me and was very selective. After the CEO suggested I get together with Hope later in the day to hear her marketing plans I tried to reassure myself the past was the past and I had learned my lesson.

Later that afternoon I met with Hope. Standing in her cubicle felt awkward and I was relieved when she suggested we grab a cup of coffee and sit outside at one of the picnic tables provided for the building tenants. I started the conversation by telling her how surprised I was to see her. After she told me she didn't believe in coincidences I paused to ponder what she meant. Smiling with a twinkle in her eye she said she had read about me in an article in the San Jose Mercury News about the movers and shakers of Silicon Valley. Flattered, I tried to remember if I had ever told her my last name.

Without me asking, Hope volunteered that after graduating from San Jose State she got her Masters from Cal. Then she went to work for a start-up and later married the founder. Their marriage lasted a couple of years before they divorced. Ironically she added their marriage ended when her husband cheated on her. When she asked about my life I nonchalantly told her business and family were both great. When I started to ask her questions about the marketing plan she smiled, looked me straight in the eye and gave me somewhat of a confession.

"You know you were different, don't you? I needed the money back then but you were different. I wish we had met in a different context when we were both single. Intelligence has always been the biggest turn on for me. I hope our past doesn't affect your analysis because this Company really has something that's going to be very big and I think I'd really enjoy working with you."

As I swallowed hard she made a smooth transition to her marketing plan. She really did know what she was talking about and I was impressed by her answers to my questions. The trouble started when I needed help figuring out a spread sheet she handed to me. To point out what I was missing she walked behind me, leaned over my shoulder and casually pressed her breasts against me as she circled some numbers with a pen. When I didn't pull away she whispered what any man loves to hear in my ear.

"You were the best lover, ever. I still remember that night because you were so sweet and thoughtful and actually concerned about me. It really wasn't about the money with you. I hope you believe me. I wish you weren't married, but I also wished for the same thing years ago."

And just like that, I gave in. All it took was her hot body, beautiful face, ego boosting words and now a wildcard, her intelligence. When I suggested we finish going over the rest of her marketing plans at dinner, she smiled and answered with her voice an octave lower, "I'd love that. I can really learn so much from you."

That night I repeated the behavior I most despise in myself. To help me from thinking about what I was doing I drank most of a bottle of wine at dinner. The sex was wild and pure passion. I thought I enjoyed the evening until the moment I got into my car to drive home.

That's when whatever conscience I had repressed returned with a vengeance.

Stupidity is often defined as making the same mistake over and over again. How stupid am I since I continued the escapade with Hope for the next two months. It seemed as long as I continued to see her I perpetuated a lie I didn't have to confront. I was consumed with trying to act like everything was normal once I got home.

Finally, three days ago I stopped the madness and ended whatever Hope and I had. Now I'm left alone in my own pool of guilt to contemplate my way out of the huge hole I've dug for myself. I don't know how or where to start.

Oh Tess, I need someone to save me from myself.

Dan

August 9, 1993

Dear Tess,

I'm truly sorry and apologize for my last letter.

I was at the lowest point of my life and dumped my misery on you. Somehow writing you allows me to face my conscience and do the right thing and the night I mailed you the letter I confessed to Maggie after the kids were asleep. I'll never forget her screaming at me when I told her what I'd done.

"You stupid son-of-a bitch. Again, with that same fucking bitch. How could you jeopardize our marriage and our family? How? Tell me how? I am so fucking disappointed in you. Why Dan, why? Do you want a fucking divorce, is that what you want?"

That was the first time Maggie had ever screamed at me or said the word fuck. Then she started to cry and shake. I never wanted to hold her more but when I tried to put my arm around her she told me to keep my fucking hands off her. For what seemed like a half hour we sat motionless across from each other in the den with her sobbing and me slumped in a chair. Finally she asked me two questions I will never forget.

"Dan, do you still love me or do you want a divorce?"

And, my answer was the first step in rebuilding our marriage. I told Maggie my truth. She was the only woman I had ever loved and I couldn't imagine my life without her. I never, ever had thought of a divorce, never. I acknowledged my despicable behavior without any excuses. I admitted to my character flaws, a drinking problem and a life that often came too easy for me. I needed help, I wanted help and I wanted our relationship and our family to flourish more than anything in the world. And I'll never forget her response.

"Dan, I believe you. I'm still mad as hell and hurt so badly I can't even look at you but I want to work it out, if we can. Let's get our butts into therapy and learn how to really communicate with each other, again. But Dan, as sure as I am in saying that let me tell you something else. If you ever fuck around again, we're finished. You need to know that. No more throwing yourself at my feet asking for forgiveness. No more second chances. Understand? Am I clear?"

And that was the start of my recovery. I immediately started therapy alone and with Maggie. I also started Alcoholics Anonymous finally admitting to myself that there is no such thing as a part-time drunk. I attend meetings regularly and have been sober for almost a year.

I did have one more conversation, by phone, with Hope but only after I shared with Maggie what I needed to do. I told Hope I would never ever see her again. I tried to assure her that Rogers Schmidt's decision not to invest in her Company was strictly a business decision made in our partnership meeting and wasn't influenced in any way by our relationship. I'm not sure whether she believed me or not but we ended our conversation by wishing each other the best, and when I got home that night I shared every word of that conversation with Maggie.

Tess, I continue to learn about myself and accept my weaknesses and character flaws. I believe I now know what triggers my destructive behavior and am committed to not falling into those traps again.

I thank you for being the catalyst that gave me back my conscience.

Dan

August 9, 1994

Dear Tess,

It was a wonderful year especially welcome after two very tumultuous years.

Maggie and I are back on track and really communicating. We've also gotten back our intimacy and with the kids older we try and get a date night every weekend. Even though I've now been sober without a drink for almost two years I still go to meetings.

Business has been nothing short of fantastic. Another one of the start-ups we invested in three years ago went public with their IPO in March and it was a big payday for Rogers Schmidt. Lately, we've been overloaded with presentations from two different types of tech start-ups, Internet infrastructure and cellular phone components.

My old Stanford buddy Jeff sold his Company for $29 million. Good for him and good for Rogers Schmidt as we were one of his early investors. I had lunch with him at a recruiting session at Stanford. He's still the same guy he was at Stanford in T-shirts, jeans and sneakers. What's very refreshing is that he's totally unpretentious. Now a multi-millionaire many times over it's never been about the money for him. Maggie and I went to his wedding in April and I was honored when he asked me to be one of his ushers. His wife Bonnie, a nurse, is a sweetheart and as endearing as Jeff. She's got a five year old son from her first marriage that Jeff's crazy about. In June Jeff stopped by our office with the biggest grin on his face because they're having a baby. It's always rewarding to see good things happen to good people. After all these years we're still talking about starting our own Company.

My amazing little girl Caroline is now fifteen. Can you believe it? Her school work is way beyond me including her never ending ethical and morality questions. She wants to be a lawyer and practices on me by never losing an argument. I thought I was young graduating from high school at seventeen but she's graduating a month before her sixteenth birthday. Who does that? Of course I've been trying to steer her towards Stanford or UCLA but she wants to go east to an Ivy League school. With her grades and test scores she can go anywhere she wants.

That's the good news about Caroline. Now here's the problem. She's dating and thinks I interrogate her dates as if they're on trial, and of course she's right. A couple of weeks ago a boy shows up to take her to a movie and I started to grill him when he tells me he goes to Stanford. He's seventeen which is a much older guy for my little girl. Luckily for Caroline her mother was there to rescue her. All kidding aside, she is the smartest, sweetest daughter imaginable. She is so much like Maggie. They're not only mother and daughter but also best friends.

Ben will be thirteen in December and is still a challenge in many ways. We're thrilled the aggressive behavior he's shown in the past had not reoccurred. His biggest challenge appears to be frustration. He'll try to do something and keep trying over and over again not knowing how to express his frustration for not being able to do what he wants. It's so sad to watch and I just try to shower him with love and attention. His favorite person in the world is Caroline and Maggie and I are worried about how her going off to college will affect him.

Saint Sarah, as I call her, is pretty much in charge of our home. We've even fixed up one of our extra bedrooms for her and she stays over a couple nights a week which really helps us out.

I finally figured out that I can only run a couple times a week and Maggie sensing I needed a new challenge bought me a very cool mountain bike for my birthday. One of the partners at Rogers Schmidt and I ride on Saturday mornings.

We saw a very different concert last month. We flew down to LA and took both sets of parents to see The Three Tenors at Dodger Stadium. There must have been 50,000 people there to hear Jose Carreras, Placido Domingo and the incomparable Luciano Pavarotti. They were backed up by the L.A. Philharmonic, L.A. Opera Chorus and conductor Zubin Mehta. It was a beautiful summer evening and really a great show. It was also the first concert I've ever seen with my parents.

Looking back this really was a wonderful year. As always, I wish you good health, lots of happiness and the realization of your dreams.

Dan

August 9, 1995

Hi Tess,

My little girl is going to Yale.

After we visited Harvard, Yale, and Princeton she chose Yale. How can we disagree with her choice since it's always rated one of the top three colleges in the country? She also likes the city of New Haven, but will live on campus as do most Yale undergraduates. The best way for us to fly there from here is through Hartford or Boston. Maggie is going back with her in a couple of weeks to help her get settled.

I couldn't be any prouder of my beautiful daughter. She is mature way beyond her years. Her June graduation ceremony was one of the highlights of my life. Both sets of grandparents flew up to watch and hear their valedictorian granddaughter deliver her commencement speech, aptly titled "Why." I was seated between Ben and Maggie in the auditorium. The content of her speech was totally thought provoking and her delivery was as good as it gets. I had probably heard her practice the speech a half dozen times but she saved her best performance for when it mattered most. Unexpectedly, the moment I will cherish most and for the rest of my life occurred when she questioned unjust wars and racial and religious discrimination. To hear her wise words brought this proud father to tears and Ben seeing this put his arm around my shoulder and whispered, "Don't cry daddy, please don't cry." For so many reasons that was one of the best moments of my life.

When they called out Caroline Mae Brewster to receive her diploma our whole row stood in unison and cheered. Hearing us she couldn't help but look over and smile.

This really was Caroline's year because for her graduation gift we decided it was about time and she deserved to see some of the world. Maggie bought her a globe with a bunch of pins and we told her she could choose where she wanted to go, within reason. The other stipulation was that she had to be accompanied by another female, whose expenses we'd also cover. The woman had to be over 21 and responsible. That description sort of limited the field and there really was never any doubt who she'd choose. Maggie and Caroline had a wonderful two weeks touring London, Paris, Rome, and Florence.

Of course not everything came up roses for Caroline. With her sixteenth birthday came the obligatory driving test and lessons from dear old dad. Let's just say I'm not sure who was more nervous and I quickly found the biggest empty parking lot I could. I'm just glad she doesn't need a car at Yale.

Ben seems to be making some progress. The special education and therapy he receives provides him the best possible environment. We keep hoping a wonder drug will soon be discovered and tested but as of today any new medication is still in the experimental phase. We're still concerned over what's going to happen with Caroline away at Yale so we found a special education teacher from Ben's school who lives nearby and can help out after school when needed.

Maggie is even more active with her autism charity work and has turned into quite the prolific fund raiser. In the spring we hosted a dinner for all the Rogers Schmidt partners and she raised $100,000. The timing of the dinner was perfect as one of the tech companies we invested in had just been acquired.

I'm happy to tell you my sobriety has reached almost three years. I've also finally stopped drinking all those diet sodas. Who knows the long term effects from all those chemicals? It's water and ice tea for me and I feel much better for it. Maggie and I continue to have very busy schedules but still make time to share our days during dinner or before bed.

The parade of new companies looking for funding continues at our office. I heard some interesting stats a couple weeks ago during a seminar at Stanford. Forty million US households now have a computer with four- teen million now online and there are now forty-four million cell phone subscribers. The predictions here in the Valley are that those numbers are just the beginning. I sure hope so because that's where we're investing.

I'm very happy with the job President Clinton is doing. The country is finally being shown a Democrat can improve the economy. Of course he's very popular in the Bay area because of his efforts to eliminate discrimination against gays and also increased spending for education.

In other loose ends, yes our house is too big and I'm riding my mountain bike to work most days since we took over more space in our building that includes a small workout room with bathrooms and showers. Finally, we're blessed that everyone is healthy and I hope you are the same.

Dan

August 9, 1996

Dear Tess,

It's been quite an adjustment at the Brewster household with Caroline away at school on the other coast.

Thankfully Ben has adjusted well and although he misses his sister I think he appreciates all the additional attention he gets. Although I miss Caroline dearly it's been most difficult for Maggie with her daughter and best friend gone from the nest. Even though they talk on the phone most every day it's just not the same. Luckily we can afford to fly back there frequently and Caroline comes home for holidays or when she has some vacation time.

I'm not surprised she loves Yale and the college experience in general. It didn't take her long to get involved in all sorts of activities. Her roommate, Shelly, is from Atlanta and Caroline says they have some interesting discussions. Since law school is her ultimate objective her undergraduate major is not that important but her choice of philosophy seems like a good fit.

Ben will be fifteen in December and at 5'10" he's nearly as tall as me. All the dedicated special need teachers, counselors and therapists have really helped him. Plus we've learned how to better manage his behavior. We understand so much more and can recognize early signals and address potential problems before they occur.

I'm not sure I've ever mentioned Maggie's younger brother, Henry, but he got married in May and we flew down to LA for the weekend. Unfortunately, Caroline was in the midst of finals and couldn't make it back. Maggie's parents, Susan and Rick, are not only wonderful parents but also great role models. I couldn't ask for better in-laws. Hank's new bride grew up in the San Fernando Valley and her dad works for Disney in Burbank.

They say mountain bike riding is like skiing in that you don't know you're going too fast until you fall. Well, I was going too fast at the end of a hard ride in the local hills. I was tired and careless and took a turn too fast. I always try to fall or slide on my butt but really couldn't in this case and instinctively tried to break my fall with my left hand. My gloves protected my hands so I broke my wrist, my first broken bone, ever.

Sometimes I get so involved in the business world that I don't grasp the enormity of what's happening up here. We're at the center of the technology universe and what's going on here every day is changing the world.

I've been very lucky to have been with Rogers Schmidt for almost twenty years and have been part of their growth into one of the top venture capital firms in the world. I've also made enough money for us to live comfortably for the rest of our lives which includes the fund we set-up to insure Ben would always have everything he might need should something happen to Maggie or I. Yes, my world is good, but at forty-five I think I'm ready to stretch my wings.

I probably see my brilliant friend Jeff at least once a month. He's been trying to get me involved with one of his tech ventures since our Stanford days. The idea probably makes more sense now than ever before since we have the money between us to fund the company at least until we have something of substantial value and can raise other money without giving away the store. Plus we both have proven track records and relationships that are invaluable. This is particularly relevant now because I had lunch with Jeff a couple weeks ago and, after he swore me to secrecy, gave me a one sentence teaser of his new concept that he's already started building in his head. He said, "It's where people live online that provides the latest communication platform for connecting people." The opportunity is huge; a billion dollar idea.

I shared this with Maggie and, not surprisingly, she said to follow my instincts and she'd support whatever I wanted to do. Jeff and I are going to get together in a couple of weeks and discuss things further but I'm fascinated with the idea of starting a Company with someone who's not only a friend but a friend with a brilliant mind. Bottom line is I guess I do have an ego and really would like to start something great that would also make the world a better place.

Here's a good story. Fifteen years ago we started a college fund for Caroline with 100 shares of Apple. Of course, we've added a lot to the fund since 1981 and luckily we can keep that fund intact while we wait for some of the stocks to mature. Rumor on the street is that Steve Jobs is coming back to the Company he founded. Caroline knows Jobs life story well since she wrote a paper on him that includes what he's done with NeXT Computers and Pixar. She refers to him as a true visionary. When I told her Jobs might be going back to run Apple her response was, "That's what they need. Please don't sell my shares."

Tess, I only hope you are living your dreams.

Dan

August 9, 1997

Dear Tess,

I've probably read five hundred business plans in the last twenty years and it's about time I wrote one of my own.

Jeff and I have started our own company. Our name is a play on the word "utopia." We have incorporated as "Utonica," and our tagline is "Where you live online." Our mission is "to build the dominant online community" and we will do this by creating the first totally interactive user experience with our platform of the most advanced set of totally integrated communication tools in the world. Jeff and I really are partners as we each wrote checks for $2 million to start and fund Utonica.

Leaving Rogers Schmidt was not easy. I couldn't have asked for a better working environment and leaving is bittersweet. It's also complicated because of our detailed partner's agreement which stipulates a twenty step formula for capital distribution when a partner leaves. I did have a huge advantage over the other two partners who left Rogers Schmidt in the past since I helped draft this partner exit agreement.

Over the years Rogers Schmidt became a second family to me and the other partners are all good friends. They all understand my move because most face similar opportunities. Of course I still have a vested interest in Rogers Schmidt success.

Our offices are an easy ten mile drive from the house and we've hired six techies, and two business types, one to handle operations and the other for marketing. Our goal is to have Utonica.com up and running in a year. It's an aggressive schedule but Jeff and I are both well aware of the cost more, take longer syndrome that cuts across any building project even if it is online.

I think we probably bought a house that's too big especially since Caroline's away at college. The house is so large it has an empty feeling most of the time. We could easily downsize which is an interesting dynamic since for twenty years we've been going the other way.

Ben is going to be sixteen in December and we continue to do the best we can by making his environment as stable as possible. We still stay abreast of all the autism research being done and Maggie, much more so than me, has become an expert in the field. Ben was evaluated again in June and his autism was classified as "mild."

The stories told by caring mothers and fathers in the Parents of Autistic Children's Group we meet with are so sad and frightening that they help give Maggie and I perspective. We're lucky we haven't had to deal with a very aggressive or violent child. Fortunately, we've been able to control any acts or tendencies Ben might have towards aggressive behavior which has always been my biggest worry.

We're so preoccupied with day to day challenges in raising Ben that we've neglected spending time thinking and planning his future. Now, led by the efforts of the autism non-profit we help support a series of workshops has been designed for parents that specifically deals with their child's future including employment opportunities and long-term living arrangements.

Caroline continues to flourish at Yale. I couldn't be prouder of her. It's been great having her home this summer. She really is just like her mother, from her long auburn hair, beautiful smile and thin frame to her kindness and sense of right and wrong. I am truly blessed. Tess, I hope your world is bright, happy and healthy.

Dan

August 9, 1998

Dear Tess,

Although we're slightly behind schedule the good news is that Utonica.com should be ready to launch soon. The bad news is that I'm back to 80 hour work weeks. It's different with your own company but it doesn't make my life any less hectic. I make sure I have time for Ben and Maggie but that doesn't leave much time for anything else. The biggest casualty has been my exercise which has been reduced to maybe a couple hours a week.

There's an interesting debate going on in the Valley over dotcom business models. One school of thought is to "get big fast" focusing on visitor growth. The other school of thought is that the "get big fast" model is not sustainable so you'd better figure out how you're going to make money early in the game. I'm somewhere in the middle although I probably prefer to "get big fast" and then sell the company.

Financially, Jeff and I have put more money into the company plus neither of us is taking a salary. We've hired three more programmers and also have four interns from Stanford who help us out with a wide range of things. Our techie's have been busy building our communication platform that includes webcams, e-mail, instant messaging, auctions, chat rooms, photo albums, personal ads and clubs. We've got an aggressive launch campaign that includes very funny billboards in strategic cities and also a hilarious TV commercial.

It's hard to keep anything quiet for too long in the Valley and the word is out we're building "Utonica." A little chatter mixed with a little hyperbole is always good. Even though we haven't gone live yet and are only a little more than a year old we received an offer to buy us from a major dotcom for $55 million. We quickly declined but that offer established a floor for the value of Utonica. It also lifted morale at the office sky high. Jeff and I celebrated with our wives over dinner.

It doesn't seem possible that my precious little girl is nineteen and going to graduate from Yale next June. Maggie's already invited both sets of parents and reserved hotel rooms. I'd better take two handkerchiefs for this graduation. Then it's on to law school for Caroline. This California girl turned Ivy Leaguer has the tough choice of choosing between Yale and Harvard.

Maggie and I are dialed in. Since we realize communication is an absolute necessity we find at least a half hour a day to just talk. I've now been sober for almost six years and still go to meetings like clockwork.

Autism and the fight to treat and cure it still consumes our lives. Maggie is now speaking to groups of parents who recently discovered they have an autistic child. Speaking from personal experience is a powerful tool and she's outstanding at relating and answering questions.

Ben seems to be doing well, at least according to his teachers. I still worry constantly but have accepted that is my role. I'm so concerned about the potential for aggressive behavior that I probably don't give him the freedom he needs. I brought that up at our last parents meeting and like most things dealing with autism there is no answer.

The flaws of being human now has a poster boy in our President. The Monica Lewinsky scandal threatens to taint all the good things Clinton has done and he's redefined the meaning of "sexual relations" for teenagers everywhere.

It's been ten years since I ran The Bay to Breakers and I don't miss that chaos but I do miss running and have put on weight. When I have time I'll ride my mountain bike to work and then either get a ride or take a cab home if it's dark. Its exercise, but not enough. I keep saying I'm going to go to yoga with Maggie but I've been saying that for twenty years. She insists it would be good for me and she's right. I rationalize that I'll start yoga when I also start playing golf—when I retire.

Wishing you the best,

Dan

PS: As you know well by now I'm somewhat grammatically challenged. I just wanted you to know that I'm aware of this shortcoming. I'm still confused over when to use "I" or "me," where to use a written number vs. the digit and still have problems deciding whether to capitalize Mother or father. Luckily, at the office my reports can be proofread by others.

August 9, 1999

Tess,

Utonica.com went live on January 1st with a big launch featuring billboards in a dozen major cities and a very funny TV commercial with dogs and babies. I called in some favors and we got a special segment on the business channel, CNBC. We also were all over both the financial and lifestyle pages of newspapers throughout the country.

Of course, even with a beta test run there still were some glitches. That's nothing unusual especially with a website like Utonica that's so robust. We've been very careful to build in total scalability to Utonica, meaning we have the capacity to grow very rapidly. It's been a wild ride as our registered members skyrocketed from 10,000 at the end of January to more than 750,000 by the end of June. What's been particularly gratifying is that other than our launch campaign we've spent practically nothing on advertising. All our growth has been viral.

People really like to visit Utonica, an average of twice a day, and use our FREE tools to connect and communicate with their family and friends. Then because they enjoy the user experience they tell their friends to join. And, in this new dotcom world that's the most effective way to grow.

More offers have come and Jeff and I are substantially apart on what it will take to buy Utonica, but that number keeps going up. My number is $400 million and Jeff's at $600 million. I'd expect Jeff's number to be higher since Utonica is his baby but either number is a huge amount of money. Maggie, of course, will be happy with whatever we decide. I like to say it's not all about the money but that would almost be a lie.

In March, I went to what is now my second favorite concert of all time. Part of what made the evening so special was my companion, Caroline. She was home for spring break and I was able to round up a couple of tickets for our favorite, Neil Young. I tried to get three tickets but couldn't find three together and when Maggie suggested Caroline and I go together I jumped at the opportunity to do something alone with my daughter.

Caroline was super excited when she heard I had tickets and didn't even appear to be disappointed when I told her she was going to be my date. The concert promised to be very special because it was Neil's Solo Acoustic Tour and at the grand old Paramount Theater in Oakland, an intimate three thousand seat venue.

I've probably seen Neil a dozen times since the late 60's but this was the first time Caroline had seen

Neil. Because I try to buy a t-shirt from every concert I attend Caroline had her choice of one of my Neil shirts to wear. She chose one of my favorites, a black shirt with white lettering from Rocking in the Free World. What really makes this shirt extra special are the white letters across the top back of the shirt which simply reads "FREEDOM."

What a fantastic night! Neil was unbelievable! He doesn't need anyone else! Just Neil, alone with a guitar, a harmonica and a piano are perfect. He sang most of our favorites including Cinnamon Girl, Southern Man, Philadelphia, Tell Me Why and of course, Cowgirl in the Sand. I've known the lyrics of those songs forever but Caroline was right with me as we sang along with Neil.

On the drive home I shared with Caroline that she was just a little older than her Mother was at our first concert. When I remarked, again, how much she was like her Mother she responded, "Father, you've been telling me that for as long as I can remember. When I was younger I didn't appreciate the comparison but now I love it! As long as we're handing out compliments I want to thank you for always letting me be me, and showering me with love and opportunity. I love you Daddy." And, I just melted.

Speaking of Caroline she's at Harvard Law School. How can anyone get a better education than following up Yale with Harvard? (Excuse me Stanford and UCLA) She also has her first serious boyfriend. Reed's also going to Harvard Law and is a star rower which is a big deal back there. Maggie and I met Reed a couple months ago on one of our trips back to see Caroline. He's almost too much of a good thing, very bright, very good looking and very much a good guy. But then I'm not sure Caroline has ever made a bad choice.

Maggie and I are facing a very difficult decision regarding Ben's future. We're relieved his behavior is stable but constantly question whether we're being too protective. We just don't want to put him in a situation he can't handle. We're now having conferences with Ben's teachers, counselors, therapist and doctor trying to make the best decision we can for Ben's future. If this sounds confusing it's because it is.

Tess, thirty years ago we witnessed rock history and for a few brief seconds our eyes met leaving an enduring memory in my mind I haven't been to escape. For thirty years I've written you a letter on each August 9th, never sure if you received or read any of the letters. I know it's not logical and maybe even delusional but I truly believe you received and read each letter.

You probably wonder how I kept finding your current address. First, I must thank the Post Office and their designation for "Return Address Requested." That's helped but unfortunately its only good for a limited period of time, normally a year. Realizing this, after the first letter, I relied on your Delta Gamma connection and my friends who were also DG's. Luckily your sorority, like most, wants to keep current on their sorority sisters, primarily for funding reasons although they also like to inform you ladies of reunions and acknowledge achievements. I did have to create all sorts of creative stories for why I needed your current address. Hopefully you've only had five address changes because that's all I've seen.

Tess, I hope to write you another thirty letters.

Dan

August 9, 2000

Oh Tess,
I am broken.

My beautiful precious Maggie, the only woman I have ever loved, was killed by a drunk driver in a horrific auto accident on a stormy night in February.

The accident never should have happened. My Maggie should still be with us. I'm to blame and overwhelmed by the guilt that consumes me. I was supposed to go to dinner that night with Maggie for the autism non-profit she helps support. Then at the last minute I called and told her to go ahead without me because my business meeting was running late. Maggie had to drive alone because I chose fucking business over her.

Maggie and I had a custom over many years where we'd always end our phone conversations with, "I love you." On that tragic night, intent on trying to get a few million more for Utonica, even those words "I love you" escaped me. My last words ever to Maggie were a cold, self-centered, "I've got to go." My selfishness beats down on me with relentless sadness since Maggie always believed there was so much more to life than money and business and would always gently remind me that there is no end to the word "more."

Seeking help from the horrific pain, I've been in grief counseling and therapy, both alone and with Caroline and Ben. It didn't help me at first and during my darkest hour I reached for the devil, my unwanted friend—alcohol. After a month in a drunken stupor, Caroline and my parents, God bless them, intervened. After pleading with me for two hours they luckily talked some sense into me and got me to start going back to meetings and into therapy. It's a battle everyday but I haven't had a drink since their intervention.

It has been terribly difficult for both Caroline and Ben; Caroline because she understands the senseless nature of what happened and Ben because he can't grasp what happened. Caroline has lost her Mother and her best friend. Ben lost his Mother and the person closest to him who he could always count on. I can't forgive myself for leaving my children without their Mother. That will never change.

I have many weaknesses, one of which is the inability to forgive myself. Maggie offered me forgiveness when I couldn't forgive myself. Her faith in me was greater than my faith in myself. She was so pure, so wise and so full of unconditional love. She was my moral compass. When I would want to spend outrageous amounts of money on things we didn't need she would always suggest, "Don't you think we can do better things with the money?" She lived for others and I will do my best to make sure her legacy is carried forward.

I now face many decisions. The first, of course, is Ben. He's ready to move on with the next stage of his life but what that means still has to be decided. I so miss Maggie's input and am lucky to have Caroline's help in exploring all possible options. Caroline's uncertainty is of a very different nature. She'll be finishing law school shortly and can write her own ticket job wise. I'd love to see her move back to the west coast for selfish reasons and be closer to Ben and me. As always, she'll make the best decision possible.

I'm not sure if I even want to stay in this area? We'll probably sell Utonica soon for an obscene amount of money but I've lost my passion to start another company or find the next big technology. Ironically, I face the same personal decision that I am trying to decide for Ben. What are we going to do for the rest of our lives?

No matter whom I'm with, or what I do, I feel alone. Today, all I know for sure is that whatever I do will not be money driven and I will never end a conversation with either of my children with any words other than, "I love you."

135

August 9, 2001

Dear Tess,

I apologize for last year's letter. I was consumed with self-pity, guilt and loneliness that was probably obvious from what and how I wrote. My life will never be the same without Maggie but I've finally tried to move forward.

The sale of the business was finalized last September for $842 million. The money I made is crazy and most of my profits have been endowed to what has been renamed the Margaret Brewster Autism School. Even though Caroline is only twenty-two she has agreed to oversee the foundation and disburse the proceeds from our $200 million endowment on an annual basis. I trust her, more than anyone in the world, and I know she'll do a wonderful job helping the cause her mother felt most passionate about. This is the same school Ben attended but now the school will double in size and eligibility will be based on a child's needs and not their parent's ability to pay. No child will ever be turned away for financial reasons.

Getting back to the sale of Utonica, the timing of the sale might have been near perfect. We had many offers but kept waiting because the offers kept going up. Soon after we sold, the landscape of the dotcom world changed dramatically. Gone are the days of merely trying to aggregate millions of users without any idea how you're going to make money. What's that old saying, "Better to be lucky than good."

Living in our home is hauntingly depressing and terribly lonely and I've contemplated a move back to the LA area. However, before that could happen I had three issues to resolve. First and foremost, Ben and his future, secondly, Caroline and what she intends to do and where, and finally, how could we keep my dear friend Sarah a part of our family.

I struggled and struggled with the best outcome for Ben and tried to gather as much current information as possible before making a decision. This included many hours of reading through the latest research and personal visits to a half dozen of the leading autism schools and facilities. Unfortunately there still isn't much that's new except for one very important statistic that did help me make an informed decision. The latest research estimates only about 5% of autistic adults live completely independently.

After lengthy discussions with Caroline we agreed the best solution would be to keep Ben in a school environment for at least several more years. We struggled with whether we were just kicking the can down the road and then concluded that wasn't relevant. The question then became whether to keep him at his old school or place him somewhere else. Before that decision could be made I had Caroline and Sarah to consider. Now with her law degree from Harvard Caroline has decided to take the California Bar. She also has responsibilities at the autism school that requires her to spend time in the Bay area, but her longtime boyfriend Reed is now practicing environmental law in LA and she wants to be close to him. They're thinking Santa Monica.

Finally, decisions were made. First I wouldn't sell our home. There really was no reason to sell it. After discussions with Ben's teachers and therapists we realized UCLA has a wonderful autistic program that would fulfill Ben's needs if I decided to move back to LA. Then Caroline and I had dinner with Sarah and her family to discuss our plans and how we could include her. Collectively we came up with a very creative solution. First, Sarah keeps her key to our Mountain View home and continues to maintain it. Secondly, Sarah will fly down to LA twice a month to help me. Basically, Sarah is now a fulltime employee and all her expenses will be covered. After resolving my three issues and with a great new opportunity my decision became easy.

I packed up and moved back to Southern California in February. Caroline helped me pick out a much bigger house than I need in Pacific Palisades on a bluff overlooking the ocean with a spectacular view of the Pacific. The best part of the house is it's only a few miles from Caroline, who, with a little help from dad, bought a condo in Santa Monica close to Maggie's parents. My new house is also close to my new job and Ben's new school.

Oh, I almost forget my great new opportunity. I'm back at my alma mater, UCLA, teaching, if you can believe it. I've been called a lot of things before but never Professor. Apparently the administration didn't want to overload me and felt two classes were enough for me to handle. The first, "Business Outside the Box" is an undergraduate course held in a large theater like room that seats about 250 students. Because the three hour class forces the students to endure my lecturing for too long, I've introduced some of the latest high-tech gadgets to keep them interested and awake. My second class is for grad students, "Morality in Today's Business." The twenty-four students get a chance to participate in fascinating discussions that I probably enjoy more than they do.

It's such a joy to be back in the academic world surrounded by bright, alive, inquisitive young people. The energy on campus is so infectious and the diversity among students is much greater than it was when I was a student here. I look forward to every day, every class and am grateful for the opportunity. I'm not sure I've ever told you this but I contemplated becoming a teacher before I went to Stanford to get my MBA. Now I wonder if I made the right decision.

Ben is comfortably enrolled in the UCLA autistic program and I take him to class and pick him up every day. I've also been very lucky to find one of the special need teachers who needed a little financial help. Tony is now our 24 year old live in helper. I give him free rent in our guest house plus a salary. With Sarah flying down Monday mornings through Friday afternoons twice a month, Caroline close by and both sets of grandparents visiting regularly, Ben has stability in his life and our house is much more a home.

There's another positive change in my life. Besides teaching I've also started to exercise—a lot. Not the token time I spent at the Company gym up north but a serious 2 hours a day, six days a week. It's another activity I gave up for business and another big mistake. My routine now consists of at least an hour of hard cardio a day combined with weights and yoga. Caroline jokes she wants me to do the Malibu triathlon with her next year. Maybe that will be my goal. I could swim in my pool at the house but the Olympic size pool at UCLA and their Masters program is much more inviting. What's important is that I feel better physically than I have in many, many years. One of these days I hope to have grandkids to spoil and I want to be around to see them grow-up.

I hope with all my heart that this world finds you healthy and happy. So much in my life has changed but you remain wondrously clear and timelessly beautiful.

Dan

August 9, 2002

Dear Tess,

After 9/11 our world will never be the same. Terrorism has become a real threat to world peace. Stopping these madmen, who are suicidal religious extremists, must be our security focus if we're to avoid other catastrophes.

It's great to be back in LA and everyone seems to have adjusted well. Most importantly, Ben seems to be thriving is his new environment. Tony has been a great help and, by accident, identified an exceptional artistic skill of Ben's. Tony's hobby is painting abstract seascapes and while he was painting the ocean from our backyard view he handed Ben a brush and a canvas on an easel. The result was a seascape unlike anything Tony or Caroline or I had ever seen. Now Ben and Tony can often be found painting alongside one another.

I would have thought we would have identified this talent earlier but then Ben never had the spectacular view of the

Pacific we have from our backyard. I've had a half dozen of his paintings framed and besides those hanging on our walls, Caroline and the grandparents each have a beautiful signed seascape from Ben on their walls. When Ben first saw the paintings framed and hanging on our walls his face lit up with a sense of pride that brought me to tears.

As she has all her life, Caroline continues to amaze me. She passed the Bar and has assumed her leadership role of the autism school up North. She's also doing pro-bono work for a local law firm and is teaching a philosophy class at Santa Monica Community College. I can't believe how accomplished she is at twenty-three. Reed is now her live-in fiancé and they make a wonderful couple although she seems too young to get married. But, I've thought she was too young to do all sorts of things in her life and have been proven wrong each and every time.

I love teaching and my classes always seem to fill up quickly so I guess the students enjoy them, too. It's a very different way to change the world but possibly even more satisfying than building a new product or company. I tell Caroline she helped prepare me for teaching because no one asks better questions.

I didn't do my first scheduled triathlon because I pulled a hamstring running but this year it's going to happen. At fifty-one I might be the in the best shape of my life and want to take advantage of being at the younger end of my age bracket. I now have a core group of friends who are as passionate as I am about training and it makes a big difference to have their company and support considering we train 2-4 hours a day. Exercise might be life's only positive addiction. My diet's improved, I sleep better and my doctor says I'm healthier than ever, but then again he's also one of my training partners.

Everybody keeps trying to fix me up but I haven't had the desire. I know this is corny but I always thought Maggie would be the only woman I would ever be with. Maybe someday I'll want female companionship but right now my life is very complete.

Sarah, bless her wonderful heart, has retired at eighty-one. She was with us for eighteen years and from the very first year has been part of our family. It was too ambitious of me to think she could continue to fly down here twice a month. It was just too much and in hindsight I felt badly that I even asked her. Caroline, Rick, Ben and I flew up to the Bay area to host a special retirement dinner for her. There were twenty-six of us, including her family and friends, and it was a wonderful tribute to a remarkable woman. For all the help and joy she's given us it was the least we could do to make sure she'll be comfortable for the rest of her life. I took a wonderfully touching photo of her being hugged by Ben and Caroline. One can never be reminded too often that happiness always comes back to the people in our lives.

Tess, I am forever grateful that I've been able to share so much with you.

August 9, 2003

Tess,
Tragically, my father passed away in June from a massive heart attack.

He was seventy-seven and I don't know if you remember, but he had a minor heart attack in 1977 after which he made many lifestyle changes. I'm painfully aware of his family history of heart problems and the reason I wear a heart rate monitor when I workout. My Mom's been staying with us and I'd like her to stay permanently if she'll have us although most of her world is still in the San Fernando Valley.

My Dad was always a wonderful role model. An engineer, he worked hard so his children could have opportunities. It's probably the greatest quality I learned from him followed closely by the wonderful relationship he and my Mother shared during more than fifty years of marriage. I can never remember my parents yelling or having a heated argument during my childhood and my fondest memories include how proud he was to come to my high school basketball games. I concluded his memorial service with these words, "He was a good man, a loving husband and a remarkable Father. I love you Dad."

It's a very difficult transition to go from what I've just written to the opposite end of life but here goes. A month before my Dad passed away I had the privilege of giving away what is dearest to my heart. My precious little girl married Reed. It was a small ceremony as the newlyweds wanted. Because I know my daughter so well I offered her the option of the wedding of her choice, big, small or somewhere in between. The kicker to my offer was that I would write them a check for the big wedding regardless of what they chose knowing full well Caroline would choose small and a check for the difference she'd use to support a cause both she and Reed supported.

The wedding for seventy-five guests was held at our house. The ceremony was in our backyard on a spectacular day. As usual, when it comes to Caroline, I lost it, somewhere between walking her down the grass aisle and watching her and Reed exchange their personally written wedding vows. My tears were of joy and sadness because I know seeing this day was one of Maggie's dreams. I didn't think I had any more tears left until it was time for their first dance. In honor of Maggie, they chose the Righteous Brothers Unchained Melody, the same song Maggie and I chose for our first dance at our wedding in 1976.

Caroline and my new son-in-law make a wonderful couple and, of course, I can't wait for grandkids to spoil. That day may not be too far off as they both want a big family.

Ben continues to prosper along with the sales of his paintings. He still loves to paint and it gives him the creative satisfaction he hasn't had before. There's a glint in his eyes when he shows me a new painting and the ever changing Pacific always offers him a different view. Little did I realize the thing I would savor most about this house would be the view it offered Ben.

I finally did it! I completed my first triathlon! It was the Malibu Triathlon and considered a short course consisting of a half-mile ocean swim, 18 mile bike ride and 4 mile run. My total time was 2:12 which placed me 9th in my age group. Caroline, Reed and a bunch of my training partners also did the race and it was an exhilarating day. I'm hooked and looking forward to my next race.

This Iraq War has me so aggravated. The "total bullshit" excuse that we had to take the action we did because of the threat of weapons of mass destruction has no factual basis. Here we go again. Bush and even more so Cheney and Rumsfeld have engineered this whole charade. How many Americans will die this time? Will we ever learn?

Tess, your image still visits me often and always brings a smile to my face.

Dan

August 9, 2004

Dear Tess,
As I do the math this is the thirty-fifth letter I've written you.

In hindsight I reflect back on the difficult years, the tragic years and the good years. It very much represents not only my life but the journey in everyone's life. It encompasses the full circle from birth to death, the hardships and disappointments and the celebration and achievements. I have been very lucky and extremely grateful to share it all with you.

Speaking of sharing, here's wonderful news. Caroline is pregnant and due around Thanksgiving. She's aware that her Mom had a miscarriage at twenty-seven, so Caroline, now twenty-five, has been very conscious of her lifestyle. Thankfully, her pregnancy has been without any problems and they're super excited to welcome their baby girl. I know they've been playing around with names and think I have a good idea what the baby's middle name will be.

My Mother moved back home. She appreciated my offer to stay and did for a few months until she became homesick for her home, friends and familiar surroundings. She left with my open invitation to return anytime she wants but, like me, she's very stubborn and will only return on her own terms.

I keep asking when someone is going to make a breakthrough in solving the autism puzzle. I understand the complexity and the reality that autism is not one disorder with one cause but rather a group of related disorders with many different causes but the results of studies and research has not proven very productive. Caroline is very active with the school up north and keeps me abreast of what she hears and I'm a frequent visitor to the autism research group at UCLA. I keep hoping, as I have for more than twenty years, that one day my special son will see and live in a clear unencumbered world.

For now, Ben seems stable. We're lucky Tony is still with us. Painting is Ben's favorite pastime and I'm running out of wall space. I think he's also excited for his sister/best friend to become a mom and I took a very touching photo last week with his ear against Caroline's baby bump.

I just keep finding more reasons to love teaching. For the first time I had several former graduate students come back to visit and thank me for what they had learned in my course. It was validation and it felt good.

I'm still only teaching two classes but that's enough because I'm training 3-4 hours a day. I did my second triathlon in April at Bonelli Park which is about thirty miles NE of downtown LA at the base of the San Gabriel Mountains.

It was an Olympic distance triathlon, a 1500 meter swim, 40k bike and 10k run. The swim was in the Puddingstone Reservoir. There's a big difference between swimming in the ocean and swimming in a lake. An ocean swim is more difficult because of the surf and currents. Most triathletes wear wet suits to increase buoyancy and provide warmth unless the water is really warm like in Hawaii. My total time was 3hrs, 9minutes which was about twenty minutes behind the winner of my age bracket. I did most of the race alongside one of my training buddies. My weakness continues to be swimming which is no surprise since I'm normally in the next to slowest of ten lanes at the UCLA Masters Swim Program.

The plan is to keep increasing the distance of my races and my next triathlon is going to be a half Ironman which is a 1.2 mile swim, 56 mile bike and 13.1 mile run. This might even be a better distance for me since there's more of a bias towards the bike and run.

When are we going to stop the madness in Iraq? Every day more and more Americans are killed. Every day more and more innocent Iraqi citizens are killed. Please, enough already.

Finally, I had a fascinating conversation with one of my fellow professors. Actually, she's an English Lit Prof who also swims in the Masters Program. She remarked how I talk in "numbers." When I asked her to explain further she indicated I use numbers as a point of reference—often. Nobody's ever made that comment to me and it got me thinking. She's right. I do think in numbers, all the time, and I probably sprinkle numbers relating to business, money, races, wars, autism, ages, concerts and most other topics when I speak or write. I just hope all those numbers haven't bored you these past thirty-five years. I think you know by now, I'm no Shakespeare.

Tess, as always I wish you the best.

Dan

August 9, 2005

Hi Tess,

It was a memorable Thanksgiving holiday.

On November 24th, the Wednesday before Thanksgiving, precious Emily Margaret Stone was welcomed into this world. The best news is both Mother and daughter had a healthy, relatively smooth delivery and both continue to flourish. I can't imagine a more appropriate time to give thanks for the miracle of life. Reed, the proud papa passed out candy cigars as the combined families filled up the UCLA Medical Center's aptly named BirthPlace. Proud and smiling grandparents, great grandparents, aunts, uncles and friends shared hugs and high-fives.

Now, more than eight months later Emily is an absolute bundle of joy. She reminds me so much of Caroline at this age. She is curious about everything and always smiling. Her parents don't have to worry about spoiling her because her grandparents and great grandparents have already taken care of that.

Not surprisingly Caroline has been extremely diligent tracking Emily's behavior almost from day one looking for any signs of autism. Thank God, there have been none. Emily, or Em, as she has been nicknamed, has passed all her baby milestones with flying colors.

Unfortunately, I can't seem to get past my bittersweet reactions to what are wonderful, life defining events like Caroline's wedding and now the birth of Emily. I always reflect on how Maggie had so looked forward to these wonderful occasions and how she's not here to share and cherish them. I've been told by a therapist friend that the pain will lessen with time but it's been more than five years since she passed away and still no relief.

We had some very welcome houseguests this spring. My dear friend, and former partner Jeff, and his beautiful wife Bonnie came down for a visit. Their two sons stayed with their grandparents in the Bay area giving Jeff and Bonnie some alone time and also some time with me. The longer I know Jeff the more I realize he really is a visionary. Now he's pretty much his own venture capital firm investing is all sorts of cutting edge technology including sustainable energy and wireless social connectivity. I still marvel that despite all his wealth and success he remains the most unpretentious person I know. The jeans, t-shirts and shorts are still his wardrobe of choice and although he has a Lexus sedan and Lexus SUV, both are more than five years old.

Bonnie remains the ultimate nurturer and compliments Jeff perfectly.

We had a wonderful time visiting the nearby Getty Museum and I took them to sit in on one of my classes at UCLA. We ate at some great restaurants and barbecued at the house one evening. It was great to spend time with them and there was nothing better than just sitting and talking. It was a great visit with best friends I love dearly.

I finally succumbed to all the pressure from my family and friends and went out on a date. Ann is a beautiful, very fit divorcee who occasionally swims at the UCLA Masters Program. One of my training buddies has been trying to fix us up for almost a year. To say my social skills have deteriorated would be a gross understatement.

Before we actually went out we had coffee together. Caroline had prepped me on how to act and I showered Ann with lots of compliments and asked her lots of questions about herself. That's how I discovered her favorite group was Coldplay. I did a little online research and found out Coldplay was on tour, called Ann and asked if she'd like to see them. They weren't appearing in LA but did have a concert in San Francisco. Ann was excited to see them and I gave her the option of either flying home after the concert or staying the night at my place in the Bay area. She opted for staying the night and seemed particularly impressed I had actually listened to her about Coldplay.

The concert was in May at the legendary Fillmore. We flew up in the afternoon, rented a car and had a wonderful dinner before watching a great concert. Since I really wasn't that familiar with Coldplay I did my homework before the concert and was pleased to discover the band members are also social activists.

There's really nothing negative I can say about Ann. In her late forties, with two kids in college she is an absolute knockout who looks fifteen years younger. She also has a sharp wit and a very playful sense of humor. It was also very flattering that she seemed very interested in me.

We really enjoyed the concert and decided to stay overnight at my house. That was a mistake. It's been hard enough for me to get past Maggie and being in her house with another woman quickly changed my mood. I tried to camouflage my feelings but Ann really wanted to play and I'm afraid I was Dan the Downer.

After breakfast and during the drive to the airport Ann brought up my mood change and was really very understanding after I explained and apologized for what happened. We went out a couple more times but there just didn't seem to be a lot of chemistry. Or, trying to be more objective since Ann really is a great catch, I still after five years haven't gotten past Maggie.

I can cross off finishing a half-Ironman triathlon from my bucket list. On March 19th a couple of my training buddies and I drove down to Camp Pendleton which is a large marine base along the coast that separates Orange and San Diego counties. The total distance of a half-Ironman is always 70.3 miles. It was a 1.2 mile ocean swim starting at the Oceanside Harbor followed by a 56 mile bike leg and then a half marathon or 13.1 miles. It was the hardest physical challenge of my life. My final time was 6hrs, 42minutes and the last five miles of the run were brutal with my legs continually cramping. I'm glad I did it but now I'm not sure I ever want to do a full Ironman which is twice the distance. The experience brought me back to my brief stint with the UCLA basketball team and how I realized I was trying to compete way beyond my talent and ability. I think I may have reached that level with triathlons.

Hope you had a wonderful year.

Dan

August 9, 2006

Dear Tess,

It has been a challenging year.

The question surrounding Ben's future continues to weigh heavily on my mind. My son will be twenty-five in December and although his life has stabilized and improved I want so much more for him. Unfortunately, autism remains a conundrum. I am extremely fortunate to be able to afford the best help, the best schools and the best doctors for Ben, but that's still not enough and I keep struggling trying to find more.

After almost five years Tony, Ben's teacher and live-in friend, has moved on. He's taken a new teaching job and also moved into an apartment with his girlfriend. He is so conscientious and so fond of Ben that he wouldn't leave until he found someone to take his place. Phil is a younger version of Tony and Ben has taken to him very quickly. The most difficult part of the transition was Phil's lack of painting skills until we realized he really didn't have to paint well but just hang-out with Ben while he was painting.

Speaking of Ben's painting, I've framed and passed out a couple dozen of his best works to friends and colleagues who all seem to really love them. A couple of the professors even suggested they have commercial value particularly for offices that want a quiet environment. It's something I need to explore.

I still keep hoping and waiting for a major breakthrough in the treatment or cure of autism and I keep being disappointed. Caroline works tirelessly with the school that bears her Mother's name but her patience is infinitely better than mine. She keeps telling me "someday" will come. For me, "someday," is too long to wait.

Our beloved friend and family member, Sarah, has been struck with Alzheimer's. At first her family thought her forgetfulness was just part of getting old but when she really started having problems remembering things from one hour to the next and started to struggle putting coherent sentences together they took her to the doctor.

Caroline and I flew up to visit Sarah and her family and also check out several recommended Alzheimer's facilities. After touring several with Sarah's family we decided on the most appropriate choice that we're convinced will give her the best possible care. We also met with Sarah's doctor who explained how patients regress over time and how the day will probably come when Sarah won't recognize us. That will be a very difficult day. Before Caroline and I left we made sure Sarah and her family will never see a bill.

Thankfully, Caroline, Rick and Emily are prospering. Most importantly, little Em hasn't displayed any signs of autism. When I hold her in my arms she loves me to read to her and, of course, I just melt. My Mom is slowing down and I drive out to see her at least once a week. She, stubbornly, is still driving and tries to visit Caroline and her great grand-daughter once a week but I'm thinking of hiring a driver for her when I'm not available.

My social life is slow, but that's okay. Caroline keeps pushing me towards online dating but finding available attractive women isn't my problem. My life is full and I'm resigned to the reality that if and when the time is right I'll seek female companionship.

Tragically, the debacle in Iraq continues and thousands of people continue to die each month. I often wonder what happened to America's conscience.

Tess, I hope this adventure we call life continues to find you healthy and happy.

Dan

August 9, 2007

Hi Tess,

I'm going to be a grandfather, again!

Caroline and Reed are expecting a boy in January. They've wanted to have their kids reasonably close in age and Em will be 3 in November. Now, their two bedroom condo is too small. I remember those days. They're looking for a bigger home in Santa Monica. The housing market, after a huge period of appreciation, is spiraling down very quickly and they may have a problem selling their condo but that's where Dad can help. I'll make sure they get their new home.

Ben Brewster is now a commercial artist. With the help of Caroline we've placed what we're calling BenScapes in the portfolios of two well known office designers in LA. Apparently there really is a market for Ben's type of paintings. They're described as peaceful and relaxing and work best in doctor, dentists and therapists' offices. The money is secondary to the self-esteem

Ben now feels and it's also given him a purpose. These are personality traits most of us take for granted but it's been wonderful to see Ben experience those feelings for the first time.

There's more good Ben news. Phil is wonderful and as with Tony it's a real relief for me to know Ben's in capable hands. The best way to describe Ben's behavior is stable and considering the other options that's a positive.

No triathlons for me this past year. Two very different injuries substantially reduced my training. First I pulled a hamstring foolishly sprinting at the end of a 10 mile training run. Because I couldn't run I started to swim more only to hurt my rotator cuff. Luckily I still had my bike to ride. Then to break the monotony of riding the highways I bought another new mountain bike. It's so convenient to walk out my front door, hop on my new bike and hit the trails of the Santa Monica Mountains just up the street.

Now, having substantially reduced my exercise routine I realize how much I miss two huge benefits other than the physical. First, I miss the camaraderie and the friendships that flourish from all the time spent training. Secondly, I miss all the time in the pool and on the roads that allows me to clear my mind and make better choices.

My already inflated ego got another boost when my students rated me a 4.5 out of 5 in an anonymous online survey of UCLA professors set up by a student group. There was an optional remarks section and they ranged from hilarious to very flattering to a little depressing. My favorite was from a student who asked, "How can this man be single? If I was 30 years older I'd be all over him!" I only hope a female student wrote this.

Guess that's as good a lead-in as I'm going to get into my social life. I have been dating, a little. At least I took out two women this past year. My M.O. seems to be dinner and either a concert or movie. Maybe I'm finally coming out of my funk because I'm actually enjoying the female companionship. With Caroline's help I've picked up lots of good pointers for evaluating compatibility. It's no secret she wants me to meet someone, fall in love and remarry. I can try to argue with her but as it's been since she was a little girl it's an argument I can't win especially when she plays her trump card, "You know Mother would want that for you."

One of the concerts I saw with a date was Rod Stewart at the Staples Center in March. He's such a showman and he puts on an incredible show with so many songs everyone knows and sings along with him. He sang my favorites, Tonight's The Night, Have I Told You Lately and of course Maggie May.

Last month I flew up to the Bay area to meet Caroline and then visit Sarah. It was so, so sad. This wonderful, sweet woman who is like a family member didn't remember either of us. Although her doctor prepared us a year ago for this eventuality it still left us feeling devastated.

After more than four years we're still fighting a senseless war in Iraq with no end in sight. I was invited to a fund raiser for Senator Barack Obama of Illinois who has White House aspirations. If he clearly advocates stopping the senseless killing and ending this crazy war he'll get my support and vote.

Tess, please be healthy and happy.

Dan

August 9, 2008

Dear Tess,

On January 2nd, Caroline gave birth to Nicolas Theodore Stone.

As with Emily the pregnancy and delivery went without a hitch and once again the entire family was at the UCLA Medical Center to welcome our latest addition. I don't know where Reed finds those candy cigars but he passed them out again.

With a real estate market that's still tanking and buyer's finding it very difficult to qualify for a jumbo loan Caroline and Reed thought they might be stuck in their small condo even though they found a new house they loved. When they showed me the 5 bedroom, 4 bathroom, two story craftsman style home in a beautiful area of Santa Monica, I too, thought it was perfect for their growing family.

A week later I asked them to show me the house again. As we drove up Caroline yelled, "They sold it, there's a sold sign on it!" Then, as we were getting ready to drive away a Mercedes drove up. It was the listing broker. I insisted we all get out of the car and find out from the broker who bought the house and when it was sold. As we approached her she opened her purse and pulled out a set of keys. She only said one word before pandemonium broke out. Looking directly at Reed and Caroline she held out the keys and said, "Congratulations!"

One of the joys of my life is sharing all I can with my family and those I love. This house was a no brainer. The day after I saw it for the first time I met with the broker and worked out an all cash deal with the title in Caroline and Reed's names. The day after they were handed the keys, armed with all the dimensions, Dad took his beautiful daughter and handsome son-in-law out for a furniture shopping spree. The thought that kept running through my mind as I bought the house and the furniture was how proud Maggie would be of what I had done.

As she did with Em, Caroline had Nick (the obvious choice for his nickname) tested for possible autism symptoms as soon as he was old enough. She was particularly concerned because the pattern was the same as with Ben, a boy followed the first child who was a girl. Thank God there are absolutely no irregular behavioral disorders and Nick is a perfectly healthy baby boy.

Hopefully we're going to have a new President named Barack Obama. Although I've been disappointed he hasn't taken a stronger stance on keeping us out of wars, and getting us out of Iraq immediately, he's certainly the only sane option considering our other choice is war hawk McCain. Besides, how can I not support a guy who graduated from Harvard Law and there's no question he's a very bright man with a beautiful family. It's also about time we had a President of color.

Assuming he wins, he's going to inherit a real mess. Our economy is probably in the worse shape since the Great Depression and correcting that humongous problem is going to be like trying to maneuver an aircraft carrier through a slalom course.

I've been training but not racing and surprisingly I'm thinking of an Ironman triathlon next year if I can qualify and my body can stand the training. I've joined a tri club and it's been a great way to meet training partners since attrition has hit my old crew.

There's also a very cute, very fit gal I met at the tri club who I've not only been training with but also dating. Sandy is an absolute sweetheart, very bright and she even laughs at my jokes. She's forty-five with one son who's a junior at UCLA. She's been divorced for three years and is great company. Like every other woman I've dated she can't believe I'm single. I'm beginning to believe what Caroline's been telling me and that maybe I really am a good catch.

Our dating pattern is to follow a great workout together with a nice dinner. I know I'm never going to find another Maggie but I'm beginning to think maybe Caroline's right and I should make myself more available. Luckily, Sandy is very understanding and is fine taking things slowly although she did say, "Will you please kiss me like you really mean it. I won't bite, oh, maybe just a little nibble." Not surprisingly, I find myself constantly aroused when I'm with Sandy which she finds very appealing. She also takes full responsibility for solving that problem.

Unfortunately it's only a matter of time until I say goodbye to my dear, dear friend, Sarah. Her mind has been taken over by the Alzheimer's. She remains one of the most loving, giving people I have ever known. She made all our lives so much better and I can't imagine what we would have done without her. I have tried to do all I can to help her and her family but it can never match the joy and happiness she gave us. I guess there's symmetry of life in this letter as I started by introducing the joy of celebrating a new life and close by my sadness of having to say goodbye to a dear friend very soon.

Tess, I have learned much in my life and now I never fight back the tears. I've also learned to celebrate all that you have meant to me.

August 9, 2009

Dear Tess,

Sadly, our beautiful friend and family member lost her battle with Alzheimer's in October. Even though we knew the day when Sarah was no longer with us was rapidly approaching it's always difficult to say goodbye for the last time.

Caroline, Reed, Ben and I all flew up for the funeral and celebration of her life. Everyone was relieved that Sarah was now at peace and suffering no longer. Caroline and I both have a large framed photograph of her being hugged by Ben, Maggie, Caroline and myself at a surprise birthday party we had for her many years ago. That photo and what it represents is how I will remember Sarah.

On the other end of the spectrum called life Em, soon to be 5 and Nick, soon to be 2, are wonderfully healthy and so much fun to spoil. I love having them so close by and I'm back to answering questions, only now with

Emily. The conversation I really enjoy is when Emily starts bombarding her Mother with probing questions. Nick is very much like his Dad. He has no fears and must go through a box of those crazy colored kid band aids a week. Reed's Mom, Carol, got out the photo albums of Reed when he was a toddler and Nick looks exactly the same.

I've assumed the role of being in charge of posting videos to the Brewster's new family Facebook page. Speaking of Facebook, three or four years ago I had an opportunity to invest in the company and passed for a reason I probably choose to forget. That decision is especially painful since Facebook founder Mark Zuckerberg fits my profile of brilliant guys who dropped out of big time colleges (Harvard) only to then change the world. Several good friends of mine from Silicon Valley did invest early on and should cash out big time when Facebook goes public.

BenScapes is now incorporated and profitable as Ben keeps churning out those beautiful abstract seascapes. The Santa Monica newspaper even did a story about him in May. They came out to the house and photographed Ben working alongside Phil in our backyard. The theme of the story was "Beyond Autism" and every week for a month a different adult with autism who has adjusted well into society was profiled. I have never been prouder of my son.

I guess you could call Sandy and I a couple, at least we're exclusive. She's a very special lady and has been very patient with me in so many ways. Her great sense of humor has helped me get past some very awkward moments. Maggie was just about the only woman I ever had sex with until recently. I don't count the casual relationships during my senior year of high school or the several college flings I had prior to meeting Maggie. Let's say they pretty much adhered to President Clinton's definition of not having sexual relations. I know I've conveniently left out the affair with Hope. That was not by accident but for reasons of guilt.

We had our first sexual encounter last September. We had dinner reservations at 7:00 and decided to go for a run about 5:00 from the house. Sandy pretty much has her own bathroom at the house but on this day she surprised me and walked into the shower with me. Besides being even hotter naked than I could ever imagine she was very playful. I tried to slow down and think of math problems or state capitals but she sort of overwhelmed me and I literally exploded. Luckily we were already very wet. When I told her it had been a long time she gave me a classic Sandy response, "I sure hope so because your powerful fire hose almost threw me into the wall. Luckily, I think I can adjust the nozzle. I'll take it as my personal responsibility" How can any man not appreciate that response?

My Ironman triathlon will have to wait another year. In February I reinjured the hamstring I've had trouble with before during a long training run. It seems hamstrings have memories of their own and I had to take a couple months off. I'm back putting in more mileage and I'll delay my first Ironman till next year.

August 9th

Unfortunately, I've been very disappointed in President Obama. Not only are we still in Iraq but now we have Afghanistan to worry about.

Happy Anniversary Tess! The wonderful memory of what I saw in your eyes for those brief seconds in Anaheim have carried and inspired me for the last forty years.

Dan

August 9, 2010

Tess,

I'm an Ironman!

I completed the Arizona Ironman in November. Although it's hard to get an entry into any Ironman race I was able to get a slot by donating a little money to the Ironman Foundation. I was thinking about waiting until I was 60 to take advantage of being on the young end of the 60-65 age group but with my cheerleaders Sandy and Caroline pushing me I decided to do it last November.

The race is double the half-Ironman or a 2.4 mile swim, 112 mile bike ride and a marathon. The original Ironman is still held in Hawaii but that's an almost impossible race to qualify for and much more demanding than the race I completed because of the heat and winds on the Big Island of Hawaii in October. The Arizona Ironman is a freshwater swim in Tempe Town

Lake, a three loop relatively flat bike ride and a flat marathon around the lake we swam in.

I took a big group for support and it turned into a great vacation. (Caroline, Reed, Emily, Nick, Ben, Phil, My Mother Laura, Sandy and me) The weather was great and we had five suites in a semi-plush resort for five days.

As to my race, it was by far the hardest thing I've ever done physically. Luckily the weather was near perfect although that didn't help my always slow swim. My arms felt like jelly getting out of the water and it took me almost ten miles on the bike to really get going. At about 100 miles into the bike ride my calves started to cramp and I was passed by lots of the riders who I had worked so hard to pass during the earlier part of the bike portion of the race. When I got off the bike I was totally exhausted. I'm not sure I would have even started the run if it weren't for my cheerleading family. As I started running my legs felt like wood. They loosened up after mile 6 and I was relatively okay for the next 10 miles. That took me to mile 16 and continual leg cramping that was an absolute bitch. The last 10.2 miles were part run, but mostly walk.

Nearing the finish, I could see and hear my cheerleaders screaming. I forgot about all the pain and tried to look good and smile as I crossed the finish and heard the PA announcer call out my name. Sandy wearing her running shoes was the first to greet me. Somehow I was able to stand as she wrapped her arms and legs around me.

After getting lots of hugs and congratulations I retreated to the large medical tent for a little massage. I was beyond sore and tired. For 14 hours 39 minutes and 15 seconds I gave everything I had and then some. Although I constantly drank water and electrolyte fluids during the race I couldn't get enough liquid into my body. I slowly walked out of the medical tent after my massage to greet my waiting cheerleaders. I learned you can smile regardless of how badly your body hurts.

I couldn't get comfortable that evening and barely had enough energy to cut the big rib eye steak I devoured along with a huge baked potato with probably a half lb of butter. The iced tea tasted wonderful and I toasted my cheerleaders after they toasted me.

Luckily, Sandy understands the pain of leg cramps because that night in bed I had them in both legs. She was a trooper and tried to massage them as they occurred. Unfortunately, I was even stiffer the next morning, but since we weren't flying home until the next day I relaxed in the Jacuzzi for about an hour after breakfast. Everyone hung out around the hotel pool the rest of the day drinking foo-foo drinks with umbrellas, and eating nachos and burgers.

Finishing that race was a wonderful experience and I was especially happy to share it with my family and Sandy. My goal was to finish an hour faster than I did but everyone hopes to finish their first Ironman faster than they do. It was fast enough and the pain and soreness eventually subsided. The feeling I had when crossing the finish line to see and hear my family supporting me is something I will never forget.

This is a somewhat unique letter because it's basically about one subject. Nobody died this year and there were no serious illnesses or major problems. It was a good year and I hope you enjoyed the same.

Dan

August 9, 2011

Dear Tess,

I don't feel old but I turned sixty in February.

I really didn't want a party and certainly not a big party but Caroline, bless her heart, felt otherwise and I don't argue with Caroline who also had the backing of Caroline Jr. also known as Emily. My birthday, Feb. 4th, fell on a Friday this year as did my party.

It wasn't really a surprise party since I knew the date and where it was going to be. What I didn't know was who or how many were coming. Let's see how many I can remember. First there was my family, Caroline, Ben, my Mother Laura, sister Janet, Reed, Emily, Nick, Susan and Rich. (My in-laws) Then my friends, Sarah's two children and her five grandchildren, Jeff and Bonnie, Sandy and her son David, Tony and Phil, Mark, my old UCLA friend who helped me identify you, five of the partners from Rogers Schmidt, a half dozen of my fellow UCLA faculty friends and four training buddies.

Then there was a group from the Autism School in the Bay Area and a group from the UCLA Autism Center. Add them all up and the total count was over sixty.

Caroline got the perfect sized party room at a boutique hotel in Santa Monica and had the hotel set up five round tables for dinner that were then moved for the dancing afterwards. What a wonderful celebration that was part tribute (embarrassing), part roast (hilarious), and then came the family speeches. (Tears, tears and more tears for me)

It was a wonderful evening and I was overwhelmed with love and gratitude. Caroline also got a hold of my bins of movies and videos and hired a videographer to edit them into a chronological movie. Now I know what it must be like to get a lifetime achievement award except I'm only sixty.

Throughout the entire evening I missed my Maggie. Her beautiful smiling face was in so many of the videos and she was so responsible for who I am and whatever good I've been able to do. Tess, I get very emotional every time I relive that evening and now I'm going to stop writing. Sorry.

Dan

August 9, 2012

Dear Tess,

I'm sorry for what I remember to be a very emotional and abrupt ending to last year's letter. My party was overwhelming and I felt blessed to receive such a warm and wonderful outpouring from my family and friends.

Sandy and I have stopped seeing each other. I have absolutely nothing but great things to say about her. She's a beautiful, caring, loving, fun lady. Our relationship started with both of us just wanting companionship, casual fun and the enjoyment of each other's company. I guess it's unreasonable to assume that any woman doesn't really want more. Eventually Sandy wanted a commitment besides just being exclusive. She wanted a future and for us to get married. The problem for me was I don't think I was ever in love with her. Our relationship worked because we enjoyed doing the same things, it was convenient and we had fun all the time. It's very possible my conception of love is too idealistic and I know it may sound corny but I want to believe the woman I marry is someone I can't live without. I miss Sandy and miss spending time with her doing things we both loved. I often wonder if I'm just destined to live the rest of my life alone.

My Mother, in her mid eighties, is as stubborn as I am. I've been trying to get her to move in with me for years but she continues to insist she's more than capable of taking care of herself. So far she's been right but to ease my worry or get me off her back she agreed to let me make a few safety additions to her house like handrails in her bathroom and a central control box for operating everything from her TV to the lights and sprinklers. She also let me upgrade her alarm system that now includes a smart button that attaches to her watch to notify the security system's office when she needs help. Also, besides her housekeeper, who comes twice a week, I hired a food service to deliver her hot dinners Monday through Friday. I guess I should be happy she's still active and healthy.

BenScapes continues to grow and is now being sold everywhere thanks to the new website. Tony runs the small business we've set up and Ben's got a printed catalog as well as the website. All he has to do is keep painting which he still seems to love. Yet again, I'm totally frustrated over the lack of new treatments or a cure for autism. Caroline, as she always does, tells me to be patient because there isn't a simple solution.

The grandkids are great and keep me busy. Em will be 7 in November and Nick will be 4 in January. I've got more toys and stuff for them to play with at my house than Caroline and Reed have at theirs. They've told me they have no more room and to keep everything I buy at my place. I continue to take pride in spoiling my grandchildren.

After all the hard training, the long hours and painful injuries I really cut back on my training and racing. I still get in the UCLA pool a couple of times a week, run once or twice a week and go for maybe a 40 mile bike ride but nothing like I used to do. After completing the Ironman I have no desire to ever do it again so I took up an activity I was saving till I got older, golf. Plus I'm more into yoga.

Practicing yoga has been nothing but beneficial. My flexibility sucked at first and it took a while, but after six months I gained a little flexibility, improved my self confidence and stopped embarrassing myself. I take classes at UCLA three times a week and although I'll never strike some of those difficult poses with the crazy names, my flexibility and balance have improved.

Golf is a different challenge and a lot more mental than I anticipated. It's also another activity that humbled me. After months of lessons, hitting thousands of balls on the range and probably playing 50 rounds I'm still below average but now, at least, I know what I should be doing. If I break 100 it's a good day, and on the rare occasion I break 90 I save my scorecard.

I have two major tech stories for you. The first was the sad passing of Steve Jobs in October of 2011. He really was a visionary and business giant who changed the world of computers, music delivery, cellular phones and even animated movies. All the people I know who knew him said the same thing, absolutely brilliant but very difficult to work with. After his passing, Carolyn asked me if she should sell her Apple stock that was now worth a lot of money. I asked her how important she thought Jobs was to Apple? She sold the stock.

The second big event was the IPO of Facebook which made tons of money for a number of my friends up North. The magic of Facebook is twofold. First it connects people in an ingenious way and secondly it is unbelievably addictive. I should know since you can put me in that addictive group.

Finally, thank God the Iraq War is finally over. I have yet to hear a coherent justification for what we did. The numbers are staggering: 4,500 Americans killed, 100,000 Iraqi lives lost at a cost of $800 billion.

Luckily, everything else in my little part of the world is just fine. I hope your world is smiling.

August 9, 2013

Dear Tess,

Can you believe Caroline and Ben are now in their early thirties; Em will be eight in November and Nick will be five in January? In retrospect, time really does fly.

The grandkids are so much fun and I enjoy every moment I spend with them. Em is just like her Mother and wants to know why her nickname can't just be the letter "M?" I'll let Caroline answer that question. Nick climbs, rides or jumps on everything. He should automatically put his helmet on whenever he goes outdoors.

In December Caroline received a special award for her tireless efforts to fight autism from the City of San Francisco. Her acceptance speech was, not unexpectedly, brilliant. I've suggested she consider politics and she didn't say no which was encouraging. I could see her running for something in Santa Monica when the kids get a little older. Reed is already one of the top environmental lawyers in the state.

Speaking of politics, I was approached by some friends who wanted me to run for the State Senate. I was flattered but passed, only to later have second thoughts. Considering my opposition to the insane wars we get involved in, Afghanistan being the latest, maybe I should instead run for the U.S. Congress? Not surprisingly, Caroline thought it was a great idea. The biggest negative for me would be all the time away from my family assuming I had a chance to win. I'm not sure I could or want to do that at this stage of my life.

I have to share a remarkable dream I had since you were part of it. Here's what probably set-up my dream. After yoga one day I heard a couple of women talking about Led Zeppelin. They told me to go to YouTube and type in "The Kennedy Center Honors, Led Zeppelin, Stairway to Heaven" and then sit back and enjoy one of the great rock performances of all time. So I did and they were right.

Plant, Page and Jones were honorees and were seated in the balcony with their wives and the President and First Lady. Performers who honored them by singing their songs included the Foo Fighters, Kid Rock, Lenny Kravitz and Heart. It was Heart's Ann and Nancy Wilson who brought the house down and tears to the eyes of the three living Zeppelin band members.

The Wilson's came out on the darkened stage alone as one beam of light highlighted them. Ann sang with Nancy on guitar and they were soon joined by a wonderful orchestra featuring drummer Jason Bonham, the son of deceased Zeppelin drummer John Bonham. But, there was more. In the middle of the song the lights to the side of the orchestra came on to reveal a choir reminiscent of a gospel choir in church. Then near the climax of the song the lights behind the orchestra came on to showcase another ninety member choir. The result was a magical finish and probably one of the great rock performances I've ever seen.

And that takes me to my dream. I was at the Kennedy Center Honors that night but this time with Caroline at my side and in the row in front of us, just as it was more than forty years ago, sat a woman with your same beautiful hair. As the audience stood to applaud the performers after Stairway the entire audience except one person turned to the balcony to salute Led Zeppelin. That one person was me and I didn't turn until I saw the beautiful face, amazing smile and unforgettable eyes of the woman in the row in front of me.

Tess, the older I get the more I realize that magic, captured in a memory, really is timeless.

Dan

August 9, 2014

My Dearest Tess,

Since 1970, on this day of the year, I have sent you a letter. Remarkably, your name, addresses and that you were a Delta Gamma at UCSB is really all I know about you. Yet, the image of your smiling face and sparkling eyes that I saw twice for just a few seconds in Anaheim forty-five years ago is as vivid and clear today as it was then.

Somehow, someway you've taught me more about life than anyone, except for Maggie. With time I realized the letters I wrote to you were also letters meant for me. The reflection and the perspective helped guide me through the ups and downs, successes and failures and joys and sorrows of a very full life.

Maggie and I were blessed with two wonderful children and she, without much help from me, raised them into outstanding individuals. I am saddened beyond belief that she is not here to enjoy her two grandkids.

My priorities, my values, my character have often been flawed and misdirected but Maggie was my compass who always patiently waited for me to find the right direction and my truth. My life changed forever the night Maggie was killed. The emptiness, the sadness, and the guilt have never left me.

Tess, although we have never spoken and I have never received a response to any of my letters you have taught me much about three of life's most mystifying subjects: hope, magic and timelessness. I'm not sure I believed or even thought much about these as a twenty year old in 1969. Today, however, at sixty-four, I believe and think often of all three.

It's no accident I have never written about love and us. Early on I was confused and didn't really know what to think or write, but with time it became clear the feelings I have for you are unique and of a different context then I have ever felt. Perhaps love was the fantasy but I always had that in my life with Maggie.

When Maggie passed I wrote a letter to you suggesting and hoping you'd agree to meet, but I could never mail that letter. My conscience, my truth kept reminding me with unmistakable clarity that I could not disrespect Maggie. That being said, I know Maggie would have been the first person to tell me to contact you but I have never had her strength and without her I could never take that step.

Tess, I am not well. I am writing you from the intensive care unit at the UCLA Medical Center. I'm dying of a terrible cancer that has overcome my body. At the beginning of the year I was diagnosed with advanced pancreatic cancer. Any symptoms I may have had were camouflaged and nothing seemed irregular until the pain in my abdomen became severe. Since diagnosed I have endured surgeries, radiation, chemo and have even been a participant in clinical trials for experimental treatments. When death is the prognosis, one will try anything.

There is no stronger human instinct than the will to survive but my pain and the suffering it is causing my family is unbearable. Over the last few days I've had personal conversations with those I love. It has been the most difficult thing I have ever done in my life but I had so much gratitude to personally deliver. When Ben and Caroline came into my room a couple hours ago my physical pain suddenly disappeared only to be replaced by the emotional pain that quickly overwhelmed me. As Caroline and Ben held my hands I became a sobbing mess. Then, as first Caroline and then Ben kissed my forehead I could endure no more pain and shut down. I don't know how long I was asleep but I awoke to my wonderful, beautiful children still holding my hands.

Tess, my doctors are amazed I've lived this long but they haven't had the benefit or the magic of my calendar with August 9ᵗʰ circled. Now my hand can write no more and I've had to have a nurse help me finish this letter. Tess, I have willed myself to stay at least until today so I could finish your letter.

With my family at my side as I close my eyes for the very last time I hope to see two images. First, Maggie, the amazing love of my life waiting for me to walk her down the aisle as my wife and partner, for all eternity. Then, I will see your beautiful face, your magical eyes and your incredible smile that symbolically speaks and forever reminds me of the best that is human. And, those two images will be more than enough.

With all my love, forever,

Daniel

August 14, 2014

*A*s Tess walked to the entrance of the Ronald Reagan UCLA Medical Center she felt a shortness of breath and started to get chills despite the hot summer day. Taking a moment to collect herself she rested her black leather case on the sidewalk and took three deep breaths, raising and shrugging her shoulders with each.

After she wiped the beads of perspiration from her forehead, she twirled her shoulder length platinum blonde hair into a little bun, picked up her black case and walked through the front door. Searching the wall directory she found the ICU floor and proceeded to the elevators. As the sliding door opened to the Intensive Care Unit Tess was welcomed by an intercom on the wall adjacent to the clouded glass doors. After reading the instructions Tess pressed the intercom button.

"Hello, how can I help you?"

"Good morning, I'm here to visit Daniel Brewster."

"Your name, please?"

"Tess or Theresa Walker, I mean Davis, I mean Tess Davis Walker."

"Thank you, Mrs. Walker. We'll be right with you."

In less than a minute the door opened and a nurse walked out carrying a file.

"Mrs. Walker, I'm Rachel Salter. I'm an ICU supervising nurse. Please, can we sit down?"

Tess pulled the handkerchief out of her pocket. She was too late. Nurse Salter told her Daniel had passed away five days earlier on the evening of August 9th.

"I'm so, so sorry Mrs. Walker. I see your name, Tess Davis, was on the list of approved visitors for Professor Brewster. As you obviously know, he was a very special man. He had to dictate part of your letter to me after he lost the use of his hands. It was the most romantic and also the saddest thing I've ever heard. He made me promise I wouldn't talk to anyone about the letter. I could barely continue to write when tears started streaming down my face. He was with us in ICU for several weeks and fought courageously until the very end. He told me he had to stay alive until August 9th, and he did. You were so very special to Professor Brewster."

A sobbing Tess softly responded, "He was beyond special and helped shape my life. I owe him so much and was here to thank him, finally, in person. Now I'm too late to share so much with the man who shared so much of his life with me."

"I'm so, so sorry. Do you know about the Memorial? It's this afternoon at his home. It's a celebration of his amazing life and all the good he's done for so many. Let me get you the directions."

—〰—

Tess drove by the address to find cars everywhere forcing her to park three blocks away. Carrying her black leather case she was drawn to the Memorial by the sounds of Led Zeppelin that kept rising in volume as she approached the big, beautiful two story home reminiscent of Kevin Kline's Big Chill house.

Young children played on the swings hanging from the two large trees in the front yard and groups of people sat around small tables on the front porch. Most everyone seemed to be in t-shirts from rock concerts, running races or triathlons. There were even a few people wearing t-shirts with beautiful seascapes with BenScapes printed under the image. Tess hoped she didn't stick out any more than she felt in her dark jeans and white silk blouse.

As she walked into the open front door she was immediately struck by the uniformity of expressions on the collage of faces. Laughter and smiles were attached to a wide range of ages, body types and skin colors. She paused at a table with a guest book, picked up the pen and then placed it back down without signing.

Tess was bewildered and uncomfortable. What was she doing there? What did she expect to find or discover? It was a mistake. There was no reason for her to be there. She had never met, never even spoken to the man whose life was being celebrated. How could she ever explain who she was and describe her relationship with Dan. She was living a crazy unfulfilled fantasy. It was too late, impossibly too late. She turned around and started to walk out when Led Zeppelin's song Communication Breakdown began playing over the speakers. It was the encore song played forty-five years earlier when her eyes focused on Daniel for the second and last time. Trembling, tears running down her cheeks, she sat on the corner of a couch and tried to gain her composure.

As she looked around she felt surrounded by the familiar faces of people she'd never met but knew so well from Dan's letters. The walls were indeed full of Ben's beautiful paintings and the big screen TVs played Daniel's home videos.

The tap on her shoulder was soft but intentional. As she turned around she was startled to be met with a similar feeling that had buckled her knees forty-five years earlier. The eyes of the woman now kneeling before her were remarkably the same, just as she remembered. For what seemed like several minutes they just stared into each other's eyes.

"He knew you would come. He knew you would come."

"Oh Caroline, you're as beautiful as your father always described you. Your eyes, those deep blue eyes are identical to his—just as I remember."

Tess couldn't hold back the emotions that had been accumulating for more than four decades. Instinctively, the younger woman tightly held Tess's hand and whispered in her ear.

"Tess, I can't even imagine what this is like for you. I'm so happy you're here. Dad knew, somehow he knew that you would come. You're so much like my father described and that's remarkable since he saw you for just seconds more than forty-five years ago. I have so much to share with you. Please, take my hand. I'd like to take you to his special place."

As they weaved their way through what must have been two hundred people they walked past the large pool to several oversized wooden chairs on the bluff that overlooked a beautiful panoramic view of the Pacific.

"Tess, this was my father's favorite spot in the world. He said it cleared his mind and fed his soul. He would just sit here and consume the world for hours on end."

"Oh Caroline, I'm so sorry I wasn't able to get here in time. I was in Europe until yesterday. After I read your dad's letter I became an emotional mess and contemplated what I should do. Then I drove to JFK and caught a flight to LA. Ever since that night in Anaheim forty-five years ago I've wanted to meet the man who had so magically touched me. But, I could never ever be the other woman and your father loved your mother with all his heart. Unfortunately, I've never found that love."

When Tess opened up the black leather case she had been firmly holding under her arm tears rolled down Caroline's cheeks. There they were—all forty-five letters.

August 9th

"I saved them all, Caroline, each and every one. The story they tell is of a wonderful man, living an incredible life filled with joy, success, love and tragedy. It was a remarkable journey. His evolution and how he described it, once a year on August 9th, was fascinating. I eagerly awaited every letter and always made sure the post office had my address changes. Caroline, I'd like to share the letters with you, if you'd allow me."

Still sobbing, Caroline whispered, "Not now, Tess, not today, maybe someday, but just not today. They were intended for you and perhaps it should stay that way."

"Caroline, I'm sure you know this but you were always so very special to your father. He continually wrote of your brilliance and how very proud he was of you. After meeting you I can obviously see why. He also commented repeatedly how much you were like your mother. His love for Ben always came with the frustration he couldn't do more to help his son. He felt his biggest responsibility in life was to insure his son was always taken care of and never a burden to anyone."

"Caroline, for more than four decades I was connected in the most unique way with your father. We never met, never spoke and only looked at each other for a few seconds, yet miraculously I could always feel his presence. In my darkest hours he somehow gave me light and hope. For forty-five years our relationship confused me but it was always a wonderful blessing."

"Tess, in just the few minutes we've talked it's unbelievable to me that dad knew exactly who you were. I think he wanted to tell me about you but didn't know how. But, I already knew his secret."

"My Mother was an incredible woman and very spiritually connected, much more so than Dad. She shared my Father's secret with me during a walk one day. We were having a rather deep conversation about forgiveness. Somehow she discovered one of your letters around the house. She sensed my father was writing letters to himself as well as you. She knew Dad loved her completely and unconditionally and felt their love was so true she could always forgive him. She told me how their marriage had survived Dad's infidelity, alcoholism and workaholic behavior. She chose never to bring up his secret or you, and never did. She didn't want to spoil something so special to him. Oh Tess, I miss her so."

"Caroline, there was never a letter where your father didn't speak of his never ending love for your mother. He never doubted she was the woman he'd share the rest of his life with. The letter your father wrote after she tragically passed described the most beautiful, most touching, most wonderful love story I've ever known. After I received that letter I really wanted to visit your dad and just hold him and perhaps selfishly ignite the magic we had shared. I even bought a plane ticket but then rationalized it wasn't the right thing to do and I couldn't and didn't take that flight. I reasoned the relationship your father and I had, whatever it was, had long ago been defined and I accepted that's the way it should stay. The timeless image of each other we shared connected us and our lives forever and I didn't have the courage to risk losing that magical perfection."

"Tess, would you like to meet my brother Ben?"

"I think I already know him and I don't think now is the best time."

"I have so many questions. What about your family, your life?"

"Oh Caroline, let's just say my life has been rather calm and relatively uninter...., nowhere near as fascinating or significant as your fathers. Let's leave it at that, at least for now." Okay?"

"Of course, but I hope we can stay in touch."

"I hope so too Caroline, perhaps once a year. August 9th seems appropriate and would make your father smile."

The two women, holding hands, walked slowly back through the house where poetically the Righteous Brothers Unchained Melody was now playing. Tears flowed down the cheeks of both women as they walked the three blocks to Tess's rented car. Then for a moment they silently stood and tightly hugged. As Tess opened the car door she reached into the back pocket of her jeans until she felt a small piece of cardboard that she pulled out and gently squeezed into Caroline's hand.

Tears ran down Caroline's face that were met by a faint smile as she looked down at the small piece of cardboard in her hand.

Tess gently closed the car door and started the engine as Caroline stared motionless from the curb. Then Tess realized she had forgotten something. She opened her black case which was on the passenger's seat and from the inner flap pulled out an envelope addressed to Daniel Brewster. Rolling down her window she called out to Caroline.

"Caroline, I almost forgot something. I want you to have this. It's a letter I wrote to your father right after I received his last letter. Then I realized I couldn't mail this letter. I wasn't strong enough to visit your Dad after you Mother died, but I wasn't going to make that same mistake twice. I had to fly out and visit him. I know it's impossible to explain the feeling your father and I shared but I hope my letter helps explain what you father meant to me. If, but only if..."

Epilogue

Dearest Daniel,

I am saddened beyond belief, in tears as I write this and hopeful with all my being that there is a miracle out there with your name on it.

Where and how do I start this letter? On every August 9th for the past forty-five years you've shared yourself with me. I have received, read and reread countless times every letter that now fills a folder in the safest place in my home.

Although you know nothing of me, I know so very much about you for I have read your story and followed your journey. I know you as an extraordinarily good man with a wonderfully giving heart and brilliant mind. I also know your demons, your weaknesses and all that makes you human.

I know you love a challenge and have had but one true love, your beautiful wonderful Maggie. I know that the joys of your life are now your children Caroline and Ben, and your grand children Emily and Nick. I know no matter what you've accomplished, which is beyond substantial, you have never felt more pride than when celebrating the many achievements of your children and grandchildren.

I know dealing with Ben's autism has been the single biggest frustration of your life and I also know how lucky Ben is to have you as his father. I know how many lives you have touched and made so much better. I am honored to have shared your journey. Your yearly diary gave me perspective on my own life, my path and ultimately my choices.

You have taught me so much through the years. You helped guide me out of an unhappy marriage and made me realize I was worthy of loving myself. Your parenting skills enabled me to make better decisions for how to single handedly raise my two sons. Your realignment of values gave me the impetus to leave a lucrative law practice and, with some irony, start a new career as a law professor.

Now after forty-five years I need to answer the very first question in your very first letter. Yes, yes, yes! During that August 9th concert, I too, felt something on a much deeper level than I'd ever felt before or since. That feeling, that image of you for those few seconds has never left me. I've probably started to write you a hundred letters but they were letters I could never mail. I could never be the other woman and totally understood the deep love you had for Maggie, even after her death. I've never forgotten the first sentence of your letter the year Maggie was tragically killed. You said, "I am broken."

Those three words and the pain I felt in your letter caused me to book a flight and catch a cab to JFK. Then, as I was about to board the plane I started to tremble. I couldn't take that flight. I didn't want to appear opportunistic and I was afraid I would disappoint you. I couldn't compete with your image of me from so many years before. Now, having written these words, I regret not having the courage to take that flight.

Dan, forty-five years later I'm still confused over how to explain what we felt. I'm overwhelmed with sadness over never having the strength to break my silence and describe all you have meant to me. As you can probably tell from this letter, we do share the inability to forgive ourselves. Unfortunately I've never had anyone in my life with the strength of your Maggie to help me.

Every year I would anxiously await your letter and I even became quite proficient in making sure the post office always forwarded my mail and also notified you of my address changes. I must also confess to checking you out on Facebook and Googling you although I only read a hundred of the impressive Google entries. From any point of view, Caroline is right, you are quite the catch!

As I close what will probably be my one and only letter to you I must tell you exactly how I feel at this very moment. What we felt in those brief seconds forty-five years ago took my breath away and still moves me to the core. The "what if questions" will always haunt me. And if there is more to come, in whatever form, I only hope I have the courage to approach you and catch your soul once again.

With all my love forever,
Tess

Made in the USA
Lexington, KY
05 April 2015